Barbara O'Brien was born in Lancashire and educated at a convent in Wales. At twenty-one she moved to New York, where she worked as an advertising copywriter.

After two years in the USA, she returned to England to work as a television press officer in charge of publicising a top soap opera and a leading current affairs programme. She gave up her job to write novels and has published six under the name Barbara Hart. She lives in Cheshire.

Barbara O'Brien

# LITTLE ITALY

A Historical Novel

*To Roger*

# PROLOGUE

Manchester, 1829

It had not been a good year for Archibald Bailey.

One of his mills was attacked by a mob and burned to the ground. And the House of Lords finally passed the Roman Catholic Emancipation Act.

'They're mad! Stark raving mad!' stormed Archibald, the colour rising in his cheeks turning them a flaming red. He glared round at his business friends from the Cotton Exchange, his eyes protruding angrily. They had been discussing the trial of William Corder for the murder of Maria Marten in the Red Barn, when a fellow cotton dealer and Tory squire addressed Archibald: 'I say, Bailey, have you heard the news? Those foolhardy Lords have been bounced into passing that damned Papist Relief Act. There'll be Catholics admitted to public office everywhere!'

Archibald thumped his fist on the leather armchair and glared angrily round the smoking room.

'What are they thinking of? Do they want us all to be ruled from Rome? The liberties of the British people will be totally destroyed if any Catholic is to take a seat in either house of Parliament! Mark my words, this will be the end of civilisation as we know it. It will be Bloody Mary all over again!'

Intolerance and bigotry, triggered by a deep hatred of Papists and Popery, swept around the small circle of like-minded, ultra-Protestant Manchester men. Into this seething group walked another man, one who represented the other type of Manchester man – the reforming, liberal-minded Manchester man.

He had some more unpleasant news for Archibald Bailey.

'You know that piece of land you sold, after your factory burnt down, Bailey?'

Archibald raised a quizzical eyebrow. The change of subject had made his facial colour return to normal. But not for long.

It's been bought by a priest,' he was told. 'A Catholic priest. He's going to build a Catholic church on it. Right under your nose. What do you think of that, my friend?'

The news came like a thunderbolt, rendering Archibald speechless. He felt a peptic attack coming on.

'That's a bit of bad luck, Bailey,' soothed one of his friends. 'First of all your mill is set on fire by that riotous mob, then the Papists get hold of the land!'

'I thought you said you'd got a good price for the land?' interjected a business colleague.

'Aye, so I did,' confirmed Archibald, viciously stubbing out his cigar. 'Only goes to prove that the power of Rome is stretching out to Ancoats, flooding our little town with gold from the Vatican coffers.'

The pleasant atmosphere of the day had been ruined and he felt claustrophobia closing in on him. Archibald needed to get out into the fresh air, if the polluted air in Manchester could be called fresh.

He walked out of his club and along Cross Street. Picking up his pace he strode purposefully in the direction of home – a large house on Mosley Street, one of the more salubrious areas of the town – where he lived with his wife Elizabeth and their four sons.

Archibald was not unattractive-looking for his forty years. His was an imposing presence, distinguished even. He was a proud man, often for the wrong reasons. He was proud, for instance, of the part his played – ten years previously – in 'keeping the King's Peace'. This was how he interpreted his role when, along with other cavalry officers from the Manchester Yeomanry, he charged upon an unarmed crowd assembled at St Peter's Field. A day that came to be known as Peterloo.

The air or perpetual belligerence that hovered about him, served him well in the rough, tough business world of Manchester merchants and manufacturers. It was said that his bark was worse than his bite, although that cut no ice with his workers, most of whom disliked him.

But Archibald Bailey's main problem was that he was totally lacking in charm.

Elizabeth his wife had grown used to his rough diamond ways in their fourteen years of marriage. Perhaps, he surmised, all men were the same. Perhaps all husbands demanded their 'disgusting' marital rights in the same coarse manner, growling 'Ready, Mother?', as his insisting hands worked their way under her bleached calico nightdress. The days he was bad-tempered or angry were the days she came to dread. There seemed to be only one thing that calmed him down. That thing. That disgusting thing.

Three sons in three years and a fourth two years later were evidence enough of Archibald's bad temper in the early years of their marriage. However, he seemed to have mellowed a little in recent times. His demands were less frequent, and now that their youngest son Benjamin was nine, Elizabeth believed her childbearing days were over. At thirty-nine years of age she certainly hoped so.

The evening sun was doing its best to break through the sooty clouds that constantly hung over Manchester, as Archibald made his way home. Thirty tone of soot and thirty tons of tar in every square mile of Manchester air did nothing to relieve his pent-up unspeakable anger.

There was only one way to relieve it. A wife had her duties to perform and Archibald had his rights. Sick headache or not, Elizabeth would, later that same night, hear those two dreaded words 'Ready, Mother?' It would be a night when the calico nightdress would be rendered superfluous to requirements.

It was the night when Ellen Bailey was conceived.

It was also the night in a small town in Tuscany when Pietro Falgoni was born.

# Chapter 1

He'd fallen for Domenica on a hot summer Sunday in Fizzano. Ironic really, because that's what her name meant… Sunday.

Pietro Falgoni was with a gang of friends, just hanging around the town square, ogling the dozen or so girls who were standing a short distance away pretending not to have seen the boys. It was a tradition in the small Tuscan town – the *passeggiata* hour after Sunday Mass when the young people of Fizzano walked up and down in segregated groups eyeing-up the opposite sex.

A group of girls in their Sunday dresses walked past where Pietro and his friends were standing and seemed to be in two minds as to whether or not they should repeat the exercise and walk past the boys again. One or two of the girls glanced in the boys' direction and then turned their backs on them and chatted to their friends in excited voices. Each of the boys imagined that the girls were talking about them. Pietro was wondering about one girl in particular, to his mind the prettiest of the group.

'Is that girl called Domenica? The one with the red scarf.' He tried to sound casual.

'The one with the nice breasts?' ventured his friend.

Pietro felt the colour rise in his cheeks. 'I hadn't noticed.'

'Of course you had. Watch them jiggle when she

walks.'

A couple of the younger boys sniggered.

'Go and speak to her, Pietro,' urged his friend. 'She keeps looking at you. I can tell she's dying for you to take her for a walk. Trust me, I know these things.' This boy, although only the same age as Pietro, sixteen, liked to think of himself as an experienced man-of-the-world and an authority on girls. Pietro, however, was not too keen to make a fool of himself.

'You go and speak to her if you're so sure.'

'It's you she keeps looking at,' pressed the other boy, keen to see his better-looking friend make the first move. Once one of the boys had made contact with a girl it would be much easier for the rest of the gang to stroll over in his wake.

'Go on Pietro,' urged the others.

Emboldened, he sauntered across to the group of girls, some of whom were now giggling in a most disconcerting way. Domenica, however, was standing slightly apart from the group as if she wished to distance herself from her silly friends. As he approached, she looked at him and her eyes met his. She held his gaze for a moment before dropping her eyes modestly to the ground. It was in that instant Pietro knew he was in love.

'Are you Domenica?' he asked keeping his voice as casual as he could, even though his heart was pounding fiercely under his best white cotton shirt. All the girls turned and smirked at their friend, who now looked up at him again.

'Yes,' she said, her voice soft and gentle. 'And you're Pietro, aren't you?'

He immediately felt himself relax. So it was true what his friend had said. She *was* interested in him! Why else would she know his name? And she was beautiful, the prettiest girl in Fizzano. All his old confidence came surging back. He struck a pose in front of her, running one hand through his thick black hair and jamming the other hand in his leather belt. Every inch the proud Italian male.

'Would you like to go for a walk?' he asked in the time-honoured way.

She didn't hesitate. 'No,' she answered pleasantly but firmly. 'No, thank you.' Then she turned her back on him and joined her friends, cutting him out of their circle.


It would be another twelve months before Pietro summoned up the courage to ask her again and this time she said yes.

'You were too sure of yourself,' she told him later, when they had been courting for more than a year. 'You thought every woman would fall at your feet! And I'd heard bad things about you.'

'Bad things?' he queried. 'What kind of bad things?'

'Oh, you know. About you and other girls.' She squeezed his hand teasingly as they strolled through the olive groves in the late summer evening.

'But I hadn't been walking with any of your friends, so how would they know?' Pietro was intrigued to know how he'd managed to earn a reputation as a ladies' man.

'Not in Fizzano,' she said, looking at him with her dark, melting eyes. 'In Carrara.'

'Oh, in *Carrara*,' he said, winking at her in a knowing way. 'Well, that's a different matter.'

Carrara, a town half a day's donkey ride away from Fizzano was famous for its stone and marble, and was where Pietro worked with his Uncle Enrico and cousin Nello. It was also where he had lived during the week in the three years since becoming an apprentice stonemason.

There were no girls he had been 'walking out with', in Carrara or anywhere else for that matter. But a man had his pride. Who was he to deny he had been irresistible to girls from an early age? That was the kind of reputation a hot-blooded Italian male relished – unlike the Italian girls who had to preserve their good name at all cost, keeping themselves as pure as the Blessed Virgin if they wished to make a good marriage.

Pietro's parents, like many of his friends', came from old farming stock. They ran their farms and their lives in a traditional way, bounded by the land which had been worked by their families for generations, in a landscape that had remained virtually unchanged since Roman times. Pietro's family farm was one of the larger ones in the area and included acres of arable land, a stream, a vineyard and an olive grove. The rows of vines and olive trees and the field of corn provided the family's essential staples of wine, olive oil and bread. On market days the Falgonis met their peers in the marketplace and bartered for goods and items they did not produce themselves.

Pietro's father, Alfonso, as the eldest son, had taken over the farm from his father – as he had taken over from his own father. The land continued to provide the Falgoni family with a good living. But the farm could only support one family at a time. Alfonso's two younger brothers, Luciano and Enrico, knew almost from the moment they could speak that the farm would pass to Alfonso and that they – as generations of younger brothers had done before them – would have to seek their fortunes elsewhere.

8

Alfonso's brothers had done well for themselves.

Luciano had travelled to England with a group of *figurinai*, makers and sellers of small statuettes and figurines. He had set out from the village more than twenty-five years ago with four other young men, all aged eighteen, in the company of a master, an older man known as a *padrone*. The group went by foot on a two-year journey, travelling the historical trade route through Italy and France, taking with them all the tools of their trade and being entirely self-supporting, producing small statuettes to sell as they travelled.

Enrico was a master stonemason and stone carver. He managed a stoneworks in Carrara, home of the famous white marble – the *bianchi marmi.*

It was to his Uncle Enrico that Pietro had been apprenticed at fifteen. Now, aged eighteen, he was reaching the end of his apprenticeship and would be able to earn good money as a stonemason and sculptor. He could earn enough money to save up and get married to Domenica. His own father had married at twenty and that was what Pietro intended to do also. Pietro's eldest brother, Giovanni, 24, worked on his parents' farm which he would one day take over. His other brother, Antonio, was – to his mother's delight – studying for the priesthood. Antonio was twenty-one, three years older than Pietro, and had been sent at great financial sacrifice to his parents to study in Rome. Their sister, fourteen-year-old Francesca, helped her mother in the house and kitchen.

It was now two years since Domenica had agreed to 'keep company' with Pietro. He was walking her to her parents' stone cottage, as he had done every Sunday of their courtship. This Sunday, as usual, they were strolling hand-in-hand. The feel of her small, delicate fingers encased in his strong, craftsman's hands never failed to arouse him. The hills were covered in brilliant yellow *ginestra* and the heavy scent filled the air as it wafted down into the valley. The evening was warm and sultry, perfect for love. Pietro longed to possess Domenica, to make her his own. But there were rules, unwritten rules. This they both knew. Occasionally, though, she allowed him to go a little further than the unwritten rules allowed.

When they reached the hay field he tugged her hand. 'Let's sit down for a little while.'

She smiled sweetly at him, sensually, making his pulses beat fast. She crouched down in the long grass, tucking her feet underneath her cotton skirt. Pietro remained standing, relishing those few moments when he was in an ideal viewpoint to look down the front of her blouse, the top three buttons of which had been left undone. As Domenica settled herself into a comfortable position, Pietro enjoyed a rare glimpse of his beloved's breasts.

With pounding heart he sat down next to her. He put his arms around her. She looked up at him, her pale pink mouth quivering. Pietro cupped her face with his hand and, with passion rising, kissed her on the lips. Slowly he moved his hand from her face to her neck, and even more slowly to the top of her collarbone. He hesitated for a moment. Often at this point, Domenica would pull away but today she didn't. He slid his hand cautiously down her soft, silky skin and inside her blouse. His fingers explored deeper into her bodice. Domenica gave a small moan, then her eyes fluttered open and she pulled away from him. Pietro's hand was still in her blouse, trapped against the material and the fullness of her naked breast. She removed it roughly and began to fasten the buttons, her face flushed and hot.

'It's a sin,' she said, not daring to look at him. 'A sin against the Blessed Virgin.'

Pietro said nothing. He was still thinking about the delicious feel of her sweet breast against his rough fingers.

'I will have to go to confession very, very soon,' she said, still not daring to look at him. She buttoned her blouse right up to the neck.

'That's not necessary,' Pietro said. 'I've touched you there before. It's not the first time.'

'And it will not be the first time I've had to confess it!'

Pietro began to feel uncomfortable. 'You don't tell the priest all the details, do you?' The idea of the elderly priest being given a detailed description of Pietro's private gropings was at the very least unsavoury.

'I have to,' Domenica replied miserably. 'In order to get absolution. He's bound to give me a big penance. Last time it was all the stations of the cross, on my knees. And I got a lecture on keeping myself pure.'

Pietro sighed. It was no use arguing with her. It was all part of the unwritten rules which in many ways he agreed with. He loved Domenica even more because of her virtue. This was the girl that one day he was going to marry and he certainly didn't want a whore for a wife.

Pietro found an outlet for his sexual frustration in the stone and marble he worked during the week. Using his claw-chisel he would attack the block from all directions, creating a satisfying mesh of criss-cross lines as he shaped the sculpture, turning it into a work of art. Often the sculpture would be of a female body, one whose curves he could touch and run his hands over to his heart's content as he smoothed and polished his work. Pietro's statutes were always popular and sold well – particularly his madonnas with their garments appearing to cling as if wet to the shapely figure, an infant Jesus placing one hand delicately on his sacred mother's well-formed breasts.

Pietro continued walking Domenica home.

'I'll see you next Sunday, my love,' he said as he waved goodbye, watching her slip away into her parents' house, her slim figure moving with unconscious sensuality under the thin cotton blouse and skirt. She was seventeen and still the prettiest girl in Fizzano. She blew him a kiss before opening the door, and then was gone.


He walked alone along the road through the village, passing the grey stone cottages with their identical Roman-tiled roofs. Geese and hens strayed onto the road to peck and scratch at its stony surface. After a short distance the stone surface turned into a dirt road as he left the village with its pretty medieval church and followed the curving grassy track that snaked its way upwards and towards the small hill where the Falgoni farm lay.

As he covered the distance between their two homes, Pietro dreamed of his future with Domenica as his wife. They would live in Carrara to start with, he planned, in a small cottage on the hillside near his uncle's stoneworks. He'd seen just the place that would be perfect for them. He'd even enquired about the rent and decided that once he'd finished his apprenticeship and was on proper wages, he could easily afford it. A little love nest for the two of them. Or maybe three of them. A baby would be nice, too. He knew Domenica loved children. Several children would make it a proper family, but not too many. Not as many as the Sorettis had. Even Domenica agreed her parents had far too many children – many more than they could afford. Four children, like his own family, that would be ideal. Two boys and two girls.

Pietro was deep in his daydreams as he walked down the track to the farm, his appetite for the evening meal sharpened by enticing cooking smells coming from the direction of the kitchen.

The farmhouse was large and square, built of finely-cut stone, surrounded by five massive black cypresses. The roof was shallow-pitched and under the deep eaves were small round holes cut in the stone for swallows to nest.

Pietro entered as usual by the large back door which led straight into the heart of the house, the kitchen – a high square room with a red tiled floor and a beamed ceiling. As he walked into the kitchen, there was a surprise waiting for him.

A dark-haired stranger dressed in unfamiliar clothes was sitting at the supper table with the rest of the family. He looked at least forty years old. Pietro didn't recognise the man.

His father jumped up from the table and put his arm proudly round Pietro's shoulders.

'Pietro I'd like you to meet your Uncle Luciano who has come all the way from England to see us!' His father beamed as he gave this startling piece of news to Pietro.

'Luciano, here is my son Pietro. I have been telling you about him and what a good sculptor he is.' The pride in his father's voice was touching.

'Pietro, how nice to meet you at last,' said his new-found uncle, a thick-set man with a large, bushy moustache.

His mother and his sister Francesca started to put the food on the table. They had cooked an old Tuscan favourite – a *ribollita* made from thick minestrone soup, white beans and strong Tuscan bread, sliced in layers with garlic and a little olive oil, baked in the oven. On the top his mother placed a good handful of freshly picked spring onions.

'Pietro is well-named don't you agree, Luciano?' his mother said, reeling off the story Pietro had heard her tell so many times before, as she started to serve the food. His brother Giovanni shot him a knowing look and raised his eyes in sympathy.

'Pietro, of course, means a rock. But how were we to know it would be such an appropriate name for him! After all, it could have been Antonio who was going to become a stonemason and Pietro a priest!' His mother chuckled again at the story which she must have told a hundred times. She never passed up an opportunity to mention the fact that she had a priest for a son. Pietro was convinced this was the only reason she kept telling the story. 'My son who is going to be a priest' were words she never tired of saying.

But tonight, instead of keeping the conversation on Antonio and how well he was doing with his studies in Rome, his mother seemed genuinely proud of 'her son the stonemason'. She kept up a long discourse about Pietro, her proud words aimed specifically at Luciano.

What was going on, thought Pietro uneasily? What on earth was she up to?

'Mamma, let us eat before the food goes cold!' said

Alfonso, his father, indicating she should sit down at the table and stop her fussing. His mother obeyed without protest. A man's word was law in his own house, particularly in front of the children, and certainly when visitors were present.

His father said grace and they began to eat. Pietro poured the wine and Giovanni filled the water glasses from the pitcher.

All eyes turned to Alfonso when, after a few mouthfuls of food, he considered it an appropriate moment to make a small speech.

'I want to drink to the good health of my brother, Luciano.' They all raised their glasses.

'Thank you Alfonso. And this wine is so good!' exclaimed Luciano, as he swallowed the strong red, full-bodied wine. 'I have missed the Falgoni wine so much. It is the taste of sunshine, the taste of my childhood.'

'Don't you get wine in England?' asked Pietro's mother.

'We do, Seraphina, we do,' replied Luciano, 'But not as good as this.' It was odd hearing this stranger call his mother by her Christian name. Not even his father did that. It was always Mamma, and others would call her Signora. But, of course, this man wasn't a real stranger, as Pietro had to keep reminding himself.

'Tell us about England,' ventured Francesca, impatience getting the better of her. 'How long have you been there? Are you married? Do you have children?'

'*Momento,* my little one,' chided Alfonso. 'Let your uncle finish his meal before you pester him with your questions.'

Luciano put his hand up to indicate to his brother that he was happy to talk.

'I don't know how much your Papa has told you about me, but I'll start at the beginning.' Luciano leant back in his chair, all eyes were on him. 'It was the year your Mamma and Papa were married. Such a beautiful wedding, isn't that true Seraphina? And you were the most beautiful bride in Fizzano.'

His mother blushed, becoming almost girlish. 'Luciano, you're embarrassing me!'

Alfonso joined in.

'It's true, Mamma, you were a beautiful bride, in a beautiful dress. And your father never stopped telling me how much the wedding cost him and saying how grateful I should be for your dowry!"

'That wedding day was the last time I saw my old home,' said Luciano, his voice quavering. 'It was the last time I saw my brother and his new wife … until today. As I walked away I picked up a handful of the good Tuscan earth in my hand and let it slip between my fingers. I vowed, if God spared me, I would return.' Luciano looked as if he was going to cry. There would be no shame if he did. Italian men were proud to be emotional, to shed tears. However, after a gulp of wine, Luciano pulled himself together and continued his story.

'It had been arranged that I would go to England with four other boys from the village with a *padrone*. To find our fortune, he told us. To earn lots of gold and then, eventually, to come back home to my own land, my beautiful Tuscany, and build a house and live here for the rest of my life …' His voice trailed off as his gaze wandered to the window with its view down the valley, a view that had remained unchanged since his childhood.

'Is that what you've come back for now?' enquired Francesca.

'How I wish, how I wish,' sighed Luciano. 'I have money, yes, but most of it is invested in my business ventures. I have many, many businesses,' he said proudly. 'Houses and shops and people working for me.'

'So you're a *padrone* yourself, now?' asked Francesca, eyes wide with admiration.

'Yes, that's right. It's a very, very good time to be working in England, in Manchester. It's the place where everything's happening – industries, factories, buildings, railways – there's even talk of digging a deep, wide canal that big ships could sail on, like the sea. Imagine that, being thirty miles from the sea and yet being able to sail into the town just like it was a port like La Spezia or Naples! Many rich people are living in Manchester and they all want to build beautiful houses and churches and decorate them with beautiful works of art. Beautiful *Italian* works of art,' he said. 'If you are a young man with talent, there is no limit to what you can achieve in Manchester.' He made it sound like El Dorado. Even Pietro was curious to learn more.

'Where is Manchester?' he enquired.

'Many miles north of London,' said his uncle. 'It took us two years to walk there from Italy, stopping for a while in different towns on the way. When we reached Manchester it was agreed that three of us would stay and the others would move on to find work further north. So Riccardo Di Nero and Mario Soretti and I stayed in Manchester, in a place called Ancoats.'

Pietro pricked up his ears on hearing the Soretti name.

'My girlfriend's name is Soretti, Domenica Soretti. I suppose Mario is some relative of hers?'

'Probably,' agreed Luciano. 'We've all got big families and it's hard to keep up with everybody's relatives.'

'So do you have a wife and *bambini,* Uncle?' persisted Francesca

Luciano shook his head sadly. 'No, Francesca. I've been too busy working hard, I'm afraid. So here I am, forty-three years' old and no wife, no family.'

Seraphina cleared the plates away and touched his arm gently. 'Luciano, you can share our family, you know that. It's like you were saying before Pietro came in tonight.'

'Me? What has this to do with me?' Pietro was beginning to get an inkling of what his mother was up to.

'Pietro,' she said soothingly, 'your uncle has come all the way from England to find some young men – stonemasons and sculptors – to work in Manchester. He wants the best craftsmen because they are to be working on a church, a very special church.'

'It will be called the church of St Agnes,' Luciano explained. 'One of the first Catholic churches to be built in England for hundreds of years.'

Pietro's mother came round to the back of his chair and stroked his head, like she did when he was a little boy. 'I am telling Luciano that you are the best sculptor in Carrara, a Michelangelo you are, and how he should take you back with him.'

Pietro was stunned. It had never occurred to him that his uncle's visit had anything to do with him. And now all faces were turned his way.

'Me? Go to England?' he stammered. 'You mean *walk* to England like you did? You must be crazy!'

'Hush, Pietro,' scolded his mother. 'Don't be so rude to your uncle.'

Luciano laughed at the boy's confusion. 'No, Pietro,

you won't have to walk like I did. We would go by boat from La Spezia – to Liverpool, and then by train to Manchester.'

Pietro knew the port of La Spezia. It was a few miles from the quarries and stoneworks of Carrara and from where the stone and marble was exported all over the world.

'Your mother is very keen that you should be one of the young men I take back with me,' said Luciano. 'She thinks you are capable of being in charge of the other stonemasons and apprentices.'

'I've only just finished my own apprenticeship,' protested Pietro. 'And what would Uncle Enrico say? He thinks I'll be working for him in Carrara.'

'Don't worry about that,' said Luciano. 'I was with Enrico yesterday and my brother is about to take on two more apprentices to replace you and Nello.' Nello, Enrico's son, had also just finished his apprenticeship as a stonemason. 'Enrico says he cannot afford to keep on employing time-served apprentices because he would have to pay you a lot more money than before. He is very happy for me to take Nello to England and put him in charge of the team of apprentices I've employed from Carrara and La Spezia.'

'You're going to put Nello in charge!' exploded Pietro. 'Well that's rich! I'm always the one who has to oversee *his* work. I don't wish to speak ill of my cousin, but he is one of the laziest people I've ever met!'

'Yes, your mother was telling me so,' sighed Luciano. 'But I've agreed to take Nello to England with me. He was very keen.' Luciano looked thoughtful for a moment.

'I have an idea, Pietro. If you came with us, when we

get to England, I could put you in charge. Make you chief stonemason. How does that sound to you?'

Pietro felt all eyes on him. It was as if time was standing still. He was aware of the gentle pressure of his mother's hands on his shoulders as she waited behind his chair... he could hear his sister's sharp intake of breath... he noted his brother's half-smile and his uncle's persuasive body language... he saw his father's sad eyes. And, if he had turned round and looked into the eyes of his mother, he would have seen a moistness that had not been there a moment before.

He could hardly take it all in. Him? Go to England?

'So what do you say, Pietro?' ventured his mother.

Pietro wasn't saying anything. He just stared at the table in front of him, clutching the water goblet so hard his knuckles turned white.

After a while he began to speak, but the words came out haltingly.

'I'd like to … I'd like to go to England .. but there's Domenica. I'm going to marry Domenica.' He looked anxiously across the table at his father who dismissed his concerns with a flick of the hand.

'She will wait. She will wait, Pietro,' he assured his son. 'And when you come back a rich man from England then you can marry her.'

Luciano joined in. 'And you will be rich, Pietro. There is nowhere in the world where there is so much money to be made, if you know how to do it. Let me tell you, they have men in Manchester they call "cotton barons". These are not men born to nobility, but are men who have made so much money from their cotton mills they are the richest people in Christendom!'

He beamed at Pietro and patted him on the hand in a

familial gesture.

'So, that is agreed! You will come with us!'

It was all too much for Pietro to take in. 'No it isn't agreed! I don't like the way you are making all the decisions for me! I am a man, not a boy!'

He jumped up from the table, nearly knocking his mother over, and rushed from the room. His father followed him outside.

'What are you doing, Pietro? Why are showing such disrespect to your uncle? Come back in straight away and apologise,' he ordered.

'Papa, I don't like the way he has come over here and is trying to organise my life,' said Pietro angrily. 'I want to stay here and marry Domenica and live in Carrara. That's all there is to decide.'

'Now listen here, you foolish young man.' His father's words were harsh but his voice was soft. 'Did you not understand what Luciano was saying? Soon you will have no job. Enrico cannot keep you on if he has to pay you proper wages. Jobs are hard to find. You will end up living at home on the farm, and that is where you will have to work. As a labourer, working for your brother Giovanni because the farm is going to be his. Now how do you like the sound of that?'

Pietro said nothing. They were in the courtyard and the sun had set behind the soft Tuscan hills. He looked out across the ancient landscape. His heart was full of anger and confusion. He shrugged his shoulders with ill-concealed bad humour. In his head he recognised the truth of his father's words. It was logical that he should go to England to earn a living now that he knew there was no future for him as a stonemason here at home. But logic was not the most important thing to Pietro at that particular moment. All he could think of was that his plans and dreams for a life with Domenica had been dashed.

He said nothing, struck dumb by his misery. His eyes felt red and hot as he fought back tears of frustration.

'So what is it to be?' said his father.

'I don't know,' he said, his voice resentful and sullen.

'Yes, you do know, Pietro. You have to go with Luciano.'

'You can't make me!'

His father grabbed him by the shoulders, shaking him with emotion. 'Do you think I want to send my son away? Do you think that is why I had children, to send them away? But that is how it is in Italy. We are a country with a few very rich people and many, many poor people. There is not enough work for everyone to be able to put food on their own table. Luciano is offering you a chance of a lifetime. If you let it go now, you may never get another one. You will end up as a peasant workman on someone else's farm. A peasant just like Tito Soretti.'

At the mention of Domenica's father, a man who barely scraped a living getting work on the farms around Fizzano, Pietro's shoulders slumped. He knew he was defeated.

'So be it,' he muttered gruffly.

Alfonso, close to tears, clasped his son to him.

'It's for the best,' he said, his voice quavering. 'But when you go away, Pietro, just promise me one thing. Promise me you'll come back.'

Pietro nodded, unable to trust himself to speak.

As he walked into the kitchen with his father he realised he had been naïve believing he could have saved up enough money as a stonemason in Carrara to marry Domenica. Her family were poor and there were many children, many mouths to feed. He could not look to the Sorettis for help in setting up a home. There would be no dowry, nothing. How much better, therefore, to go to England and earn the money there?

Alfonso spoke for him.

'Pietro would be honoured to go to England with you, Luciano,' he announced.

'Yes … please,' said Pietro, his voice unsteady. 'It will be a good opportunity for me to earn enough money to marry Domenica. And perhaps I will bring her to England. I can do that, can't I?'

'When you have the money, yes of course,' said his uncle soothingly.

'I will speak to her next Sunday and tell her what I am going to do,' planned Pietro.

'Ah, now that's the problem,' replied Luciano. 'The boat leaves La Spezia when it's finished loading the stone and marble. That will be on Wednesday. Then we sail to Sicily to pick up oranges and provisions for my shops – I supply several in Manchester with Italian produce from my warehouse. Then we sail for Liverpool.'

'That's only three days!' Pietro was torn. He knew he must go to England, it was an opportunity that would probably never be offered to him again. But what about Domenica? He couldn't leave without speaking to her.

His mother, who had surreptitiously dabbed her eyes on her apron, was now standing next to his father. She made a suggestion.

'Tomorrow,' she said, 'go to her house and speak to her. Why wait till next Sunday? If she loves you, Pietro, she will want you to go to England. Listen to what I say.

Listen to your Mamma.'

Tears sprung to Francesca's eyes. 'I don't want Pietro to go, Mamma! He'll forget all about us and we'll never see him again!'

Luciano reached across the table and touched her hand gently. 'That isn't true, my little one. An Italian never forgets the land of his birth. Italy will always call him back. There's a bond forged between us Italians and our land. A bond that is slender as silk but strong as steel. It is something you feel here.' He pressed his clenched fist dramatically onto his chest, over his heart. 'Always. And forever.'

And so it was arranged that Pietro Falgoni would go to England, to Manchester, to work on the sculpting and stonework of the new church in Ancoats – one of the first Catholic churches to be built in England since the Reformation. But first he had to tell Domenica that he would be leaving Italian shores.

On his way her house the next day his heart was full of mixed emotions. He was excited at the prospect of his new life and new opportunities in England – but desperately unhappy about leaving his beloved Domenica. What would she say when he told her? Would she be happy for him or angry that he was leaving her? He would have to convince her that he was definitely coming back for her, that she was his one and only love, for all time.

When he arrived at the shabby cottage door, Domenica's mother answered his knock.

'She's not here. She went over the hill to Baccani. My cousin came this morning to say they need help with my great-aunt. She will stay for a few days .. or maybe a few weeks, I can't remember exactly what was agreed.' Signora Soretti, distracted by several young children clutching at her skirts and baby screaming in her arms, was very vague about the whole matter.

'When? When did she leave?' asked Pietro frantically.

'One, maybe two hours ago.'

With his heart racing he set out on foot in the direction of Baccani, a village a few miles away from Fizzano. He was in two minds whether to go back home and fetch a donkey to make the journey quicker, but decided the sooner he got going the better. As he round a bend in the hill he saw two figures in the distance.

When he caught up with Domenica and her cousin they had nearly reached the village. Pietro asked if he could speak to Domenica alone, so the cousin continued on his own telling Domenica to catch him up later.

'How nice to see you, Pietro!' laughed Domenica, delighted to see him. 'Do you have work in Baccani?'

'No, I came to find you, my love. I have something to tell you.'

The desperate look on his face struck fear in Domenica. 'Whatever is the matter? Has someone died? Tell me what it is?'

'I have to go away. To England.'

The news did not sink in.

'You're going to England? But you'll be back soon, won't you? Is it for work you're going?'

He could tell she hadn't taken in the enormity of what he'd told her – she was reacting as if he'd said was going to Lucca or Florence or some other town in Tuscany. He decided he had to use more brutal words to get the message across. He didn't have time to let her down gently.

'Domenica, I am going to England! It's like going to the other side of the world. I may be there for a long time. A very long time. Possibly years.'

Her hand leapt to her mouth and she gave out a small cry. 'Oh!'

As her legs were about to give way she swayed towards him and he held her in his strong arms, pressing his face into her hair.

'I have no choice, my love. I have to go. When my apprenticeship is finished I will no longer have a job at the stoneworks. My uncle has just come over from England and has promised me a very good job … a job where I can earn lots of money so we can get married.'

'If you go you will never come back!' sobbed Domenica.

'Domenica, my love, my life! I will come back as soon as I can and marry you. I promise you, on the life of my mother! We will be together for always, in Italy or in England, it doesn't matter where. Just as long as we're together.'

He cupped his hand round her face and kissed her with a passion that left them both gasping for air.

'I will walk with you to your cousin's house,' said Pietro, 'but we will say goodbye now, here on the hillside. This is how I shall remember you with the soft breeze blowing in your hair, and teardrops on your beautiful eyelashes. I will kiss them away, then you must be brave and wait for me. Promise me you'll wait for me.'

'I promise, Pietro. I will wait for you forever.'


Once the boat was on its way to England, Pietro tried to

put the sadness of leaving Domenica to the back of his mind. As well as his cousin, Nello, there were half dozen other young stoneworkers his uncle had employed and they all had a lot to occupy their thoughts. Feeding on the hyperbolic stories supplied to them by Luciano, they became dizzy with excitement at the prospect that lay ahead – England! The land of opportunity, and the promise of riches beyond their wildest dreams.

# Chapter 2

The euphoria was sustained throughout the sea voyage and the novelty of the train journey to Manchester. New experiences were as numerous as the oranges they had brought with them from Sicily for Luciano's warehouse.

On his arrival in Manchester, a girl walked past Pietro and she reminded him in a vague sort of way of Domenica. With a guilty jolt he realised that he hadn't thought about Domenica for quite some days. Too many exciting and novel images had taken over in his conscious mind and distracted him from thinking about his true love.

He turned his eyes away from the girl and followed his uncle and the group of young stoneworkers out of the railway station and towards their destination.

'Ancoats. Manchester. Yes. No. Thank you.' He kept repeating these few English words to himself, practising the sound of this strange new language. The future seemed bright, which was more than could be said for the Manchester weather. The air tasted of soot and it hung like a pall around the city streets.

'Perhaps tomorrow the sun will shine?' Pietro said hopefully, catching up with Luciano.

His uncle laughed. A hollow laugh. Not like the merry laughs they'd shared together on the voyage to England.

'For all we know the sun could be shining now,' Luciano replied enigmatically.

Pietro and his companions followed Luciano along the cobbled streets of tall tenement houses with their shabby front doors opening directly onto the pavement.

'Welcome to Ancoats,' said Luciano waving his hands in an expansive gesture. Before any of the young men could make any unflattering comments – and Pietro had quite a few on the tip of his tongue – Luciano produced a sheet of paper from his pocket and began reading out names.

'Rico, come over here. You will be lodging in the next street.'

The little group carried on walking behind Luciano along the cobbled road and down a narrower street of back-to-back houses. These were the streets, Luciano told them, where the mill workers lived and where many Italians had made their homes. Washing lines were strung out across the alleyways from houses on one side to identical ones on the other. Pietro could hear the familiar babble of the Italian women as they brought in the washing that had been drying in the sooty summer's breeze. Children, some barefooted, some wearing clogs, were playing hide-and-seek, dodging under the sheets and clothes that were still left flapping on the lines.

After ducking under the lines, they reached the first address on Luciano's list – the house where Rico was going to be lodging. Luciano went up to the open door and spoke in Italian to the homely-looking woman sitting outside on a cane-backed chair. Then he introduced her to her new lodger and Rico was led away into the dark recesses of her house. This same procedure took place until only Luciano, Nello and Pietro were left.

'You boys will be staying with me at Signora Palomba's house.'

They followed their uncle to the next street and to the Italian grocery shop where Luciano had his lodgings. Uncle Luciano had a room of his own; Nello and Pietro shared another one. The motherly Signora Palomba welcomed them warmly and took the young men proudly to their room. It wasn't a large room but it was scrupulously clean and freshly white-washed. The floor was covered with a simply patterned home-made rug. Pietro was relieved to see that there were two iron-framed beds with flock mattresses as he didn't relish the idea of sharing a bed with his cousin Nello. The other piece of furniture in the room was chest of drawers and on top of it was a framed picture of the Sacred Heart.

Pietro settled into life in Ancoats reasonably quickly. He missed the sound of birds first thing in the morning. But he was very adaptable and eager to throw himself into his new life and new opportunities with vigour. His settling in was helped in no small measure by their landlady, Signora Palomba. The Signora, who had two teenage sons living with her, ran the grocery and provisions shop and looked after her lodgers well, cooking their meals and doing their cleaning and washing. It was a good arrangement and made the transfer from Italy less of an upheaval for the young men.

The day after their arrival in Ancoats, Luciano gathered all his newly imported stonemasons together and set them to work. Their first job, as he had already told them in Italy, was to work on an ambitious project conceived by an elderly Catholic priest, Father James Whitaker. They were to help build the new church of St Agnes and beautify it with intricately sculptured stonework and marble, inside and out.  It was going to the most beautiful church in Manchester, second only in magnificence to the cathedral.  It would take years of work, Luciano happily informed them.  Years of good wages, years of sending money back home to Italy if that is what they wished, or years of spending it on themselves over here in Manchester.

Years away from Domenica, thought Pietro with a sinking heart.


Father Whitaker knelt down and admired the latest addition to the magnificent high altar – a life-size figure of St Agnes, patron saint of his newly-finished church which he'd named in memory of his mother.

The main altar was made of imported French stone and Italian marble.  The side altar, dedicated to Our Lady, contained a beautiful statue of the Virgin in white Carrara marble.  The total effect of the stonework and marble was magnificent, turning the whole of the interior of the new church into a work of art.

The elderly priest was well pleased.  Every sculptured stone of that sacred pile spoke to him of obstacles overcome, of bigotry buried, of perils and persecution now thankfully in the past.  It was a monument to the 'old faith', a faith that steadfastly refused to die.

Touching the feet of St Agnes he admired the polished stone and marvelled at the craftsmanship that had gone into creating this new sculpture by the Italians sculptors he'd commissioned to do all the decorative stonework in the church.

He knelt down in front of the altar and the silver tabernacle which contained the consecrated hosts and offered a silent prayer. He thanked God that he, James Whitaker, had lived to see this day – a day when all his childhood dreams had been fulfilled. In years to come, he wondered, would the Catholics of Manchester remember how it used to be? Would they remember how, in the midst of the stormy times when their religion was proscribed, a few families kept the faith alive – handing it down to their children as it had been handed down to them? James Whitaker had been born into an old Lancashire Catholic family. His mother, Agnes, whose ancestors were landed gentry, had nurtured the forbidden faith in her only son.

To the outside world the Whitakers appeared to be a good Protestant family. They, and many others like them, were known as Church-Papists – outwardly conforming to the Church of England whilst remaining inwardly Catholic.

'We have to keep our faith a secret,' said his mother, the saintly Agnes, 'but we must never give up the fight. Remember, James, once a Catholic, always a Catholic.'

On his mother's death, James studied for the priesthood at the English College in Rome. After his ordination he stayed abroad for many years – in Italy, a land he came to love like his own. However, he had never given up the hope that one day he could practise his beloved religion openly in the land of his birth in a proper church – with bells and a steeple and a marble altar – like the churches he'd seen in Rome and Florence and Sienna.

During the time James was abroad, things began to move at a pace that would have been unimaginable only a few years before. The Catholic population in Manchester was now in the tens of thousands, a rapid increase on the days when 'official' Manchester Catholics could be counted on the fingers of one, or at most two, hands.

It took a combination of the industrial revolution and the potato famine, which resulted in huge numbers of immigrant Irish Catholics, to force through the Catholic Emancipation Act which finally removed all of the penalties and most of the restrictions. One of the restrictions that had been lifted was the law against Catholics building their own churches.

The new church of St Agnes in Ancoats had taken three years in the building, but many, many more in the planning. James had initially used part of his own inheritance to buy a plot of land, the site of a burnt out mill. He then used up the rest of his own money in building and furnishing the church in the finest Italianate style. In doing so he felt he was honouring his mother – for whom the church was named – in the most fitting way. A memory in stone.

James Whitaker was deep in thought, reliving times past, when he heard footsteps at the back of the church. Turning round he saw it was Pietro Falgoni, the young man in charge of the Italian stonemasons whose work had so beautified his simple church.

Pietro walked down towards the white-haired old priest and knelt next to him in the pew after first genuflecting and crossing himself.

'You like the new statue, Father? Issa nice?'

The priest was always enchanted hearing English spoken with an Italian accent; it was so pleasing on the ear, so melodious. He smiled back at the handsome young sculptor. Pietro's English was coming along fine. The lessons he had offered to give the lad when he arrived three years ago had been eagerly accepted. Here

was a young man who would go far, considered the priest
… further than Ancoats, which was rapidly turning into
an Italian home-from-home.

'Yes, Pietro I think it's nice.  In fact, it's more than
nice, it's magnificent.'

'I am happy with it too, Father,' said Pietro, admiring
his own work without any show of false modesty.  'But I
am sad too.  Because now my work in this church is
finished. Next week, I go somewhere else. So …'  He
shrugged his shoulders in a typically Italian gesture.

'That doesn't mean we won't see you here in the
future?' ventured the priest.  'You and all the other Italian
stoneworkers are among some of my most faithful
parishioners.  And I hope you'll still be able to serve
Mass from time to time?'

'Oh, yes,' reassured Pietro, a young man who took
great pleasure in his role as an altar server – something
he had done since he was twelve years old. Saying the
responses at Mass, using the familiar Latin words so akin
to his native Italian, reminded him that he wasn't really
so far away from home.

'I will still be living in Ancoats,' he assured.  'But I
work at big house in Nortendon for many weeks, maybe
many months.'

'Nortendon?'  queried the priest.  'Ah, Northenden.
It's lovely out there.  Lots of trees and fields and fresh
air.  You'll like it.  I wish you luck, Pietro, and good
fortune for the future.  You and your team have worked
so hard for three years to make St Agnes a church to be
proud of.  A shrine to Catholicism in Manchester.'

Pietro took his leave of Father Whitaker, formally
shaking hands in the traditional Italian way.

'I see you next Sunday, Father.'  Pietro genuflected

again and turned to walk out of the church, a place he had come to know intimately and love because he had put so much of himself into creating its beauty.

After he'd called in at the church, Pietro walked back to his lodgings. After three years he was still with Signora Palomba, still sharing a room with Nello. But unlike Nello, who spent his wages as quickly as they were handed to him, Pietro had saved every penny he could. He knew it was the only way to hasten his return to Italy and to Domenica.

Although adapting to this new life quickly, he'd found his time in England much harder than he'd imagined it would be. He missed the warmth and the sunshine and the unspoilt Italian countryside, so different from the man-made hell of the world's first industrial city. He'd had no idea how homesick he would become. Great waves of emotion and nostalgia swept over him at unexpected times and he would find his eyes filling up and a lump coming to his throat – a lump so big he could hardly swallow.

As he reached Signora Palomba's shop he heard enticing sounds coming from The Red Dragon, the public house opposite. It was a well-known and popular meeting place for the Italian men of Ancoats. Here they were able to enjoy each other's company in their noisy meetings, recreating a little of the Italian social life they so missed.

Their shouts could be heard at the opposite end of the long alleyway as they played cards and a peculiarly Italian guessing game which involved banging the palms of the hand on the table and shouting *'Uno, due, tre'*.

And that evening an Italian version of bowls was also being played outside on the road.

As he walked into The Red Dragon, Pietro recognised the booming voice of his uncle.

'Eh, Pietro, let me buy you a drink. I'm buying all my boys drinks tonight,' said Luciano, jovially. 'Tonight we celebrate completing the work on St Agnes's.'

Standing close by Luciano were several of his co-workers, including his cousin Nello. They were all beaming at Luciano, who appeared to be the most popular man in the pub that evening.

'Tomorrow you start the new job, Pietro, and I'm putting you in charge again.' Luciano winked at him, unseen by Nello, who was at his back. 'Nello, of course, is in charge of the mosaic and terrazzo workers ... they still have many more weeks to do at the new museum in Salford. *Salute!*' He handed Pietro a beer and drank his health.

'Thanks, Luciano,' said Pietro, having dropped the 'uncle' several months ago.

Pietro didn't want to be drawn into a discussion about who was in charge and who wasn't. He'd had enough of that when he first arrived and his uncle had promised both him and Nello that they would be the chief stonemason. It took several months of misunderstandings and unpleasantness between the two cousins before a compromise was agreed. Pietro was put in charge of the stoneworkers who worked on the mouldings outside the church and the delicate carving and statues inside. Nello was in charge of the group who were working on the floor tiles and the beautiful inlaid floor mosaics. As a result of their work in the new church the group had recently been commissioned to work on the floorings of several of the new prestigious Manchester buildings.

'Tell me about the new job,' said Pietro. 'Do you know the owner of the house?'

'Not the owner,' confessed Luciano, 'But I'm very friendly with the foreman. He was very impressed with the work we've done on the church. We'll take a carriage down to Northenden tomorrow and you can work out the materials you'll need.'

Over the hustle and bustle in the pub came the distinctive sounds of a barrel-piano. It was a sound that had become increasingly familiar in Manchester, as hordes of Italian boys swarmed the town's streets wheeling their musical instruments and clutching pet monkeys. Some of the Italian entertainers would carry a hurdy-gurdy, a small box on the end of a stick. Inside were violin strings activated by a wooden wheel that worked like a violin bow. The screeching noise produced by a hurdy-gurdy was described by many as a terrible racket. A much superior form of musical entertainment was created by the barrel-organs and the smaller barrel-pianos. But these gaily-painted instruments were expensive items and well beyond the pockets of most of the poorer Italian boys who often ended up working for a master. Manchester folk appreciated the touch of colour and gaiety the Italians and their musical entertainment brought to the dingy streets.

'Antonio's here!' shouted one of the men who had been playing cards. This signalled a great exodus from the pub as all the men and youths gathered round the popular figure. He looked a handsome sight, in his Tyrolese hat, red jacket, grey sash and leggings, as he turned the handle of his honky-tonk machine and treated them to a medley of well-loved Italian songs to the great appreciation of his audience.

Barefoot children, tiring of playing hide-and-seek under the flapping washing lines, gathered eagerly round him, handing the pet monkey from one to another with shrieks of delight. The men, for their part, picked up the words of the songs – songs their mothers sang to them – and chorused together through half-a-dozen old favourites.

Carlo Palomba eased his way through the good-natured crowd of compatriots. Touching Pietro lightly on the shoulder, he said:

'Mamma says to come. The meal is ready.' He gave the same instructions to Luciano and Nello and the three men downed their drinks and followed Carlo into the provisions shop and through to the back room where the Palomba family lived.

'Luigi!' called Signora Palomba up the stairs to her younger son. 'Luigi, come down this minute. Why do you always keep everyone waiting?' Pounding down the stairs came Luigi, who at fifteen was two years younger than his brother Carlo.

Once she was satisfied that all the men were seated and ready for the food, Signora Palomba began to serve the five of them. She would eat later, by herself, as she always felt uncomfortable jumping up and down from the table to serve them while trying to eat her own food at the same time.

Tonight Signora Palomba had made *cannelloni*, the pasta tubes stuffed with the best minced beef and a good helping of tomato *conserva* with a special cheese sauce.

Just like Pietro's mother used to make.

'Nello and Pietro,' she said, 'tonight we'll open a special bottle of wine to celebrate the end of your big job. Carlo, go into the shop and get a nice bottle of the best vintage chianti,' she instructed her eldest boy. 'I know you like a taste of home, isn't that true Luciano?'

One of the benefits of owning an Italian provisions shop was that she always had the best Italian ingredients to hand, including the finest imported Italian wines.

'Signora, you are too kind to us,' said Luciano who, though he had known the lady many years, still kept up the formalities when speaking to her in front of her sons and his nephews. It would never do for those impressionable young men to think there might be some intimacy or impropriety between them.

Signora Palomba was a handsome woman for her forty years. Since her husband's death she always dressed in black but with a colourful scarf covering her head in the traditional style of her homeland. Luciano had lived as a paying guest with the Palombas for many years and had become a good friend of the family. Indeed he was honoured to be chosen as godfather to their eldest daughter, Marietta.

Although Luciano found Maria Palomba attractive, he also knew that as the widow of a close friend he must show great respect for the woman. His own carnal needs were catered for by the lower class of woman, of which there was no shortage on the streets of Manchester.

'So, Pietro,' asked Carlo, opening the wine bottle, 'Where are you going to work now? Are you perhaps going back to Italy?'

'No, Carlo,' replied Pietro. 'We have a big job lined up – well quite a big job – at a big house which is being built by a rich cotton man called Mr Bailey. Very, very rich my uncle tells me.' Pietro rubbed his thumb and fingers together and gestured towards Luciano. 'Lots of money for us, I hope. Then I can afford to go back to Italy.'

'Mr Bailey certainly has lots of money, Pietro, but like all Manchester businessmen, it's no easy task getting it off him. His foreman was telling me how he has invested money in a new railway company and wants to keep down the cost of his house.'

Luciano was not stupid. If he told Pietro exactly how much he had negotiated for the job of beautifying Bailey's ugly new mansion, Pietro and Nello would be demanding a much bigger share of the loot. As it was, Luciano had many business deals on the go, and supplying stonemasons was just one of them – albeit a very lucrative one. There was so much civic and private building going on in Manchester, and a great shortage of skilled craftsmen. As a result he could charge virtually anything he wanted for the sculptors and decorative stonemasons – craft-skills that seemed to have been lost for generations in England after the Reformation.

Maria Palomba gave her two sons and the two boys – which is how she thought of Nello and Pietro – a second helping of pasta.

Of the two boys, she much preferred Pietro. He was a fine ambitious young man, tall and well-formed, with aristocratic features and a head of lustrous black hair. She would have liked Pietro for one of her daughters in a few years' time. But unfortunately he had his mind set on a girl from his own village, so that was that. Maybe Nello would do, she pondered. He wasn't too bad, after all. A little lazy perhaps, but fortunately his uncle was cracking the whip and making him get on with his work and spend less time with that rough group of friends he seemed to hang around with who were only interested in gambling and betting.

Maria was constantly on the look-out for nice Italian boys for her two daughters Marietta and Angelina. They were still only young – fifteen and twelve – but she had been planning their marriages for quite some years. She missed her girls so much. They were living in Italy with her sister, Anna and her elderly parents, and had been there since her husband, Giuseppe, had died five years ago.

Giuseppe had been many years older than Maria. He was a glass-blower and had come to Manchester from Como as a young man. After saving enough money, Giuseppe had returned home to Italy and married a girl from his village, Maria who was twenty years younger than himself. He brought her back to Manchester and purchased the Italian provisions shop in Ancoats where they lived and which she looked after. They had four children, two boys and two girls – and were a happy family. Giuseppe continued to work as a glass-blower. But in the harsh English winter of 1845, he caught pneumonia and died.

The widowed Maria Palomba struggled on alone for a while – but found she was unable to carry on with looking after the shop and the four children. Reluctantly, she sent for her sister to come and take the girls back home to Italy while she and the two boys managed to run the grocery business.

Maria planned to find husbands for her daughters from among the Italian community in Manchester so that all her family would eventually be back together again.

Perhaps she would have one more try for Pietro … he would be so right for Marietta, who was now fifteen and almost old enough to be married.

'Pietro,' she ventured, 'are you still planning to marry that girl, what's her name?' She knew exactly what her name was.

'Domenica,' replied Pietro. 'Yes, I will marry her one day.'

'But don't you think perhaps she may not have waited for you? It is three years since you last saw her. She may have married someone else, don't you think?'

That disturbing thought had occurred to Pietro many times, but it was something he kept pushing to the back of his mind. When it was put into words by Signora Palomba however, it forced Pietro to face the issue head on.

'I do hope she hasn't married someone else,' he said gloomily. 'I just don't know. I have no way of finding out, except by going back to Fizzano and knocking on her door.'

'Then why don't you,' suggested Nello, pouring himself another glass of chianti. With Pietro safely out of the way in Italy, he could take charge of all the stonemasons hired by his uncle. 'Why don't you go back on the ship that brings the Italian marble and stone?'

Pietro looked questioningly at his uncle. 'Is that possible, Luciano? Could I go back home for a short time?'

'It's a possibility,' said his uncle, thinking over the proposition. 'As a matter of fact, we need to be ordering some more supplies of Carrara stone and terrazzo tiles. And tomorrow we will need to work out the quantity of material needed for the Northenden job.'

He paused and looked at Pietro's eager face. Perhaps he should give the lad more responsibility.

'You are familiar with the kind of quality we need,' he stated, 'so it's not such a bad idea to send you over to choose them. But will you be any good at negotiating a good price? I don't want to end up paying the earth for it. Can you be a tough negotiator, Pietro, that's the question?'

'Yes, of course I can,' said Pietro, jumping at the opportunity. 'You tell me what you are prepared to pay – and I'll get it for you fifty per cent cheaper!'

# Chapter 3

The foreman in charge of the construction of the mill owner's new house was Jem Hodgins. He was a man of stout Lancashire stock, thoroughly reliable, intelligent and honest. The mill owner in question, Archibald Bailey, had plucked him from his job as an operative cotton spinner and put him in charge of all the building and works projects connected with Bailey's four mills.

When the thick blanket of smog that hung like a curse over Manchester had finally persuaded the Bailey family that they could no longer live in the centre of town, the man chosen by Archibald to oversee the building of his new, sumptuous home in the leafy Northenden countryside was Jem.

That is how, and why, these two men were to be found one summer's evening standing in the grounds of the former farm where Archibald's grand new mansion was taking shape.

'Now, what about all this stonework and the fancy bibs and bobs that Mrs Bailey's insisting upon. Have you got that sorted out?' asked Archibald impatiently.

Jem modestly assured Archibald that everything had been taken care of. In his plain, unpretentious manner which so commended him to his boss, he explained in simple language the complicated business of beautifying the rather ugly building that was now in the process of being erected.

'I've taken on some of the best stonemasons in Manchester, Mr Bailey, don't you worry about that. They're Italians – the very best craftsmen you can get. They've been doing all that fancy work on the new Royal Museum in Salford – all that twirly stonework and marble columns and that broken pot stuff on the floor.'

'Broken pot stuff? You mean mosaic?'

'Aye, that's the stuff. Looks like it's made from pieces of pots dropped on t'scullery floor. It's all the rage, so I hear.'

'Mrs Bailey certainly wants it, Jem. Like you, I don't hold with all that fancy stuff, but it keeps the ladies happy.'

'Aye,' laughed Jem, 'Miss Ellen in particular!'

It was common knowledge that old Archibald Bailey, hard man that he was, could be wrapped round the little finger of his only daughter.

The two men walked back through the field to the building site where the new house was rising like a phoenix from the ashes of an old Northenden farmhouse that had been on the site for two hundred years. They were only a few miles from the centre of Manchester with all its industrial filth, yet it could have been another world. One of the many things the foreman had learned in his dealings with Archibald Bailey was to tell him only that which he knew would please him. He therefore omitted to inform him there'd been an accident that morning in which one of the labourers got his head split open when he fell off a ladder while carrying a block of sandstone.

He also omitted to tell him that the Italian stonemasons who would be working on his house were the very same stonemasons who had worked on the new Catholic church in Ancoats.  Archibald Bailey hated Catholics even though he didn't actually know any.

'The stonemasons are coming tomorrow, Mr Bailey,' said Jem, casually.  'I'll be here to sort things out.  No need for you to bother yourself with it.'

'I shall be here, myself,' said Archibald. 'Me and Miss Ellen.  She's been nagging me for days to come and have a look at how everything's progressing.'

First thing next morning, Pietro and Luciano took a carriage to Northenden, to the house they learned was to be called Bailey's Mount.

They were met by Archibald Bailey and his foreman, Jem, who was already known to Luciano and Pietro. Jem introduced the men to his boss.  Stepping smartly forward, he announced in his best voice:

'Mr Bailey, may I hintroduce you to the two mister Falgonis – Mr Luciano and his nephew, Mr Pietro.'

The three men nodded at each other.

Standing next to Archibald Bailey was a young woman.  This was Ellen, Archibald's twenty-year old daughter – a girl who managed to hide a good deal of her plainness by dressing expensively and tastefully.  Her eyes were bright.  As Jem had not introduced her to the men, she stretched out her hand to Luciano in a confident manner.

'How do you do, I'm Ellen Bailey,' she said, much to the surprise of Jem and the obvious annoyance of her father.

'Ellen! These are *workmen*,' muttered Archibald under his breath.

His daughter ignored him, still keeping her hand outstretched and smiling warmly.

Luciano, unused to English women giving him their hands, took it reverently in his and raised it gallantly to his lips, bowing slightly in a courteous, continental way.

'It is a pleasure to meet such a beautiful young lady,' he said before letting go of her hand.

Archibald was taken aback at this 'foreign' behaviour but decided not to make an issue of it. However, he was not having that olive-skinned young lad doing the same thing as the older one.

'That's enough of that,' he said, hastily manoeuvring his daughter out of the way of the young blade, just in case he had a mind to slobber all over his daughter's fair hand. 'We English don't go in for that kind of thing. A nod of the head will do fine.'

'But Father,' protested Ellen, 'they're only being polite. And you haven't introduced *me* to these two gentlemen.'

'I keep telling you they're *workmen,* not gentlemen,' replied Archibald, his mutter becoming a snarl.

His daughter stood firm. Archibald waved wearily to Jem.

Jem repeated his formal introductions:

'Mr Bailey and Miss Ellen Bailey, may I hintroduce you to the two mister Falgonis – Mr Luciano and his nephew, Mr Pietro.'

As the men nodded again, Pietro sneaked another glance at Ellen. He noticed that she was staring at him. It was an unsettling feeling and not something he was used to. Young women in Italy would not dream of acting so boldly. Yet here was this well-brought up young Englishwoman brazenly staring him straight in the eye, scrutinising him as if he were a piece of merchandise she was considering buying.

The four men and Ellen walked over the house and garden and the Falgonis made notes of what was required for their decorative stone and marble work. Pietro noted with interest that all the ideas seemed to come from the mill owner's daughter. When suggestions were made about how they might do certain mouldings and archways, it was always Ellen who made the final decision. She even persuaded her father to commission three statues for the garden, something that hadn't been mentioned previously. And even though Luciano's English was far better than his nephew's, it was always Pietro she asked to describe how the work would look on completion, how long it would take, and so on and so forth.

It was as if she couldn't get enough of hearing him speak, watching him struggle with his broken English, marvelling at the way he moved his hands so expressively as he searched for the correct word or phrase. He began to feel embarrassed at her close scrutiny and worried that he might start blushing like a schoolgirl.

'You're the first proper Italian I've met,' she said, as if to explain her unsettling behaviour. 'Well, I don't count those Italian gypsy boys who play their hurdy-gurdys, begging for money.'

When her father was out of earshot she added, 'I think you are the kind of Italian who is portrayed in opera or art. The kind of Italian I imagine Michelangelo would have been like ... or Raphael or Leonardo da Vinci.'

Her comments, far from putting him at ease, only made him more uncomfortable. And she kept making excuses to keep him and Luciano as long as possible at Bailey's Mount, even asking about statuary for the garden.

'You never mentioned statues before,' said her father, crossly.

'I've had it in mind for some time,' she said airily. 'A garden of this size has to have some statues, Father.' Turning to Pietro she asked, 'How long would you say all this would take?'

'Never mind how long it will take, lass. Just think how much brass it's going to cost!'

'Oh, Father, you want Bailey's Mount to be the envy of all your friends, don't you? Other mill owners have gardens full of statutes!' Without waiting for his reply, Ellen asked Pietro again, 'So how long will it take?'

'I think about six months, maybe seven,' replied Pietro. 'I get my men to work very fast, but issa bigga job, issa bigga house.'

'Oh you mustn't rush,' said Ellen. 'Sculptors are artists, after all.'

Pietro noticed that Luciano was impatient to go. The carriage was waiting and would be costing money. He gave a small bow.

'*Scusi*,' he said and he went to join his uncle.

'*Andiamo*,' said Luciano when he saw Pietro was ready to leave. 'Let us go.'

Archibald turned to his daughter who was watching the departing Falgonis with rapturous attention.

'They're only workmen you know, not visiting royalty.' He sounded vexed. '*Foreign* workmen at that.'

She looked up into his eyes like she did when she was a little girl.

'I know,' she said sweetly. 'They're *Italians*... from *Italy*. Isn't that marvellous!'

# Chapter 4

After three years way from Italy, Pietro was back in the land of his birth and minutes away from seeing his beloved Domenica.

He had brought her gifts; valuable cloth from England – and flowers from his mother's garden. He'd also brought with him a heart full of anxiety. Did Domenica still love him? Had she waited for him like she'd promised she would? Last night, his mother had answered in response to Pietro's enquiry:

'I don't think Domenica is married. Not yet, anyway. There were rumours about a man, a cousin I think. You will find out tomorrow, when you visit her, whether or not she has waited for you.'

Pietro could tell that his mother was secretly hoping that Domenica was either married or about to be. She had never hidden her dislike of the whole Soretti family.

'She will have waited for me,' Pietro told his mother with a confidence he wasn't feeling.

'If she hasn't waited for you, Pietro, it's not the end of the world. I'm sure there are many other, more suitable, girls who are just dying to marry you.'

'More suitable? You mean richer?' Pietro was making a big effort not to fall out with his mother – so soon after arriving home from England. But he knew that she had never approved of choice of Domenica. In fact, he wouldn't put it passed her to have come up with the whole idea of his going to England with Luciano just to get him away from his girlfriend.

Three years ago he'd overheard his parents discussing Domenica.

'I want a bright future for Pietro,' his mother said. 'I don't want him to marry a girl from that rough-neck Soretti family with no land and no dowry. If he went away from her it could be a case of out of sight, out of mind.'

Well, his mother was wrong. Domenica might have been out of sight but, in all of those three long years in England, she had never been out of mind. He thought about her every single day as he worked in that alien, industrial environment.


Domenica Soretti at twenty was at the peak of her physical beauty. The innocent looks of her teenage years had developed into a curvaceous, smouldering sexuality – all breasts and hips, pouting lips and flashing eyes. These features were never more obvious than when she was doing the housework in her old cotton dress, its hand-sewn seams strained almost to bursting point.

Slopping the mop around the stone floor, the cooling sensation of the wet surface on the soles of her bare feet brought a moment of sensory pleasure to an otherwise dreary chore.


His daughter's burgeoning womanhood was one of the many things that troubled Tito Soretti. He needed to get her married and off his hands. It wasn't decent, it wasn't comfortable, to have this voluptuous young woman still living under his roof when in the natural run of events she would have been given in marriage at least two years ago. If he waited much longer before marrying her off it might be too late. Italian country women, in his personal experience, tended to go downhill pretty quickly after blossoming and ripening nicely at around nineteen or twenty. His own wife, Maria, certainly had. Her shapely figure and pretty features coarsened at a frighteningly rapid rate, it seemed to him. Having nine children in quick succession had no doubt added to the acceleration, but it was something that concerned him about his eldest daughter nevertheless.

Tito's cousin, Angelo, had shown interest in marrying Domenica. But the girl was so stubborn. She insisted she was promised to that Falgoni boy, the one who had gone away to England three years ago and had never come back. Three years is a long time to keep his daughter waiting, concluded Tito. Tonight, when he came in from the fields, he was determined to have a show-down with the girl. She must be made to marry his cousin – or else.

Angelo, a short, sturdy, beetle-browed Sicilian, had arrived injured on their doorstep two years ago. How or why his cousin had received his injuries was a mystery to Tito. He told Tito and Maria that he was a freedom-fighter, and said they were not to ask questions. It wasn't important.

What was important was the fact that he was family. Family always sticks together.

Angelo was half-dead when they found him. It was only through Domenica's constant and devoted nursing that he survived.

He was thirty-two, several years younger than Tito. After several months – when he had recovered from his injuries – Angelo worked as a peasant farm labourer like Tito and his three sons. The house where they all lived was small and crowded. It was bad enough before Angelo arrived – the older children crowded into one bedroom, a curtain dividing the girls' sleeping area from the boys', and the youngest sleeping with their parents.

The injured Angelo was nursed on a straw mattress on the kitchen floor. But when he recovered he too joined the three Soretti boys in their cramped sleeping area, all four sleeping in one large double bed, two at the top, two at the bottom.


'Shoo, shoo,' said Domenica to her two youngest sisters who were about to run with their dirty, dusty feet onto her newly-washed kitchen floor. 'Outside, you two. Go to Mamma.'

'We want to come in, 'Menica,' pleaded the four-year-old. 'We want to jump on Uncle Angelo's bed.'

'Shhh!' cautioned their big sister, putting her finger to her lips in warning. 'You mustn't tell anyone I let you do that!'

Their little faces crumbled. The five-year-old stuck her lip out in disappointment. These two little moppets knew how to melt their big sister's heart.

'Alright then,' she said, lifting them over the clean floor and pointing them in the direction of the boys' sleeping area and its massive double bed that was even bigger than the one in her parents' room.

Domenica, like most Italians, loved children and she longed to have *bambini* of her own. She squeezed out the wet mop and sighed. When would she marry and have her own children? Was she being foolish waiting for Pietro who left so suddenly and without any warning? Would he ever come back? Meanwhile, there was a man who had asked her father if he could marry her. A man who was short, squat and coarse-mannered. Cousin Angelo.

It had been different when she was nursing him. She had felt great tenderness towards him. He was so ill, so vulnerable. She tended to his every need, dressing his wounds, washing and feeding him, like she would a sick child. Her mother had been rather shocked at the suggestion that Domenica, an unmarried girl, should deal so intimately with the bodily needs of a man.

'It's not decent,' she complained to her husband. 'It will ruin Domenica's reputation. What will people say when they learn she is touching a man all over his body, with only a small piece of cloth covering his ... well you know what I mean.'

It was something that had worried Tito, too, but there were other over-riding considerations. 'Angelo is family, Mamma. How would it look if we rejected our own flesh and blood? A Sicilian can always look to his own for protection. You, Mamma, are unable to look after him, you have all your own children and a husband to care for. No, it is for Domenica to do it. There will be no problem if she nurses him. No disgrace.'

Bringing disgrace on the family was a major concern. Italian men, particularly Sicilians, could carry a vendetta down from one generation to another, taking revenge on those who brought dishonour to their family name.

For weeks, Angelo hovered between life and death as infection spread through his wounds. For months afterwards he remained weak and helpless.

When he started his slow recovery Domenica would spend many hours alone with him. He would tell her about life in the village in Sicily where her grandparents used to live. It was a rougher, harder lifestyle than the one she had experienced in Tuscany. No wonder her father had left the island and settled further north.

And yet Angelo said he yearned to return home – but only when the land was free – when all the Italian states had kicked out their hated foreign rulers. His fighting political talk both fascinated and frightened Domenica. Once the need for her nursing skills had abated, she still liked to spend time with him. He stimulated her intellectually, speaking to her in his Sicilian dialect about people and places and events she had never in her narrow experience of life heard discussed before.

But while Angelo was stimulating her mentally, it was obvious she was stimulating him in a totally different direction. His eyes were forever wandering to her shapely hips and rounded buttocks. His rough, workman's hands itched to encircle her tiny waist, then slide slowly down over the delicious swell of her womanly thighs. Many times she would catch him looking at her in a way that frightened her and made her feel unsafe alone in his company. And so in recent weeks she had made sure she was never on her own with him, especially after her father had told her Angelo wanted to marry her. Her Papa had said she should accept the offer because she might not get another one. Girls without a dowry couldn't be choosers, he told her. Two days ago she overheard her parents arguing about it.

'*You* make her marry him, Mamma. You tell her how nice it is to be married. How she can have lots of babies and be happy like you are.'

Her mother snorted in disgust. 'Babies, that's all you men can think of! I'm worn out with having babies.'

'So don't mention the babies! Tell her she can have her own house to clean instead of cleaning this one. Tell her anything, only get her married to Angelo. I have another five daughters to marry off. If we have an old, unmarried daughter living in the same house nobody will look at the next one.'

The whoops of the two little ones jumping up and down on the boys' bed was becoming a little too noisy and would get them all into trouble if they were discovered.

'Right, you two,' said Domenica, picking one little tousled-haired girl under each arm and depositing them outside the back door. 'Now, off!' She patted each on the bottom, propelling them into the back yard where the washing was drying on the line.

Stepping back into the house, she heard a knock at the other door, the one that opened onto the street.

A look of sheer delight came over Pietro's face when he saw it was Domenica who opened the door to him. They each stood there staring at one another, saying nothing just smiling foolishly basking in the thrill of the moment.

'I've come back,' said Pietro, thrusting a bunch of flowers and a brown-paper package into the hands of his beloved. 'For you. From England.'

Domenica looked in disbelief at the flowers. 'From England?'

'Oh, no,' corrected Pietro. 'Not the flowers. The cloth, in the package.'

Domenica looked with excitement at the parcel that

she was holding and ran over to the kitchen table to open it. Pietro followed her, standing closely by, slipping an arm round her slender waist.

She undid the string and opened the paper, revealing a large folded piece of printed cotton, the best Pietro could buy.

'Oh, Pietro,' she gasped, holding up the blue-and-yellow print material against her. 'It's beautiful. I have never seen any material like this. It is so fine, so soft.' She pulled it round her waist. 'I will make a new skirt and wear it with a white blouse,' she said excitedly. 'Do you think that will look nice? Will it look good on me, Pietro?'

Pietro couldn't take his eyes off her, she was so lovely. Even more lovely than when he had left three years ago. She was now a woman, not just a pretty girl. A beautiful, sensual, seductive woman.

'Yes, Domenica,' he said huskily. 'It looks good on you. It is the new printed calico from Manchester. From the cotton mills of Manchester, the best in the world.'

She flung her arms round Pietro. 'Thank you, Pietro. Thank you for the present and thank you for coming back to me.'

The scent of her hair, the touch of her cheek on his … Pietro was transported back to the days of their courtship. Domenica felt it too, and all the years of waiting and longing broke down her instinctive reservation. They kissed with a passion and fervour like never before.

'Have you come back for me?' she said desperately in his ear, running her hands through his hair, enflaming him with the intensity of her desire.

'I came back because I need to know that you are still my girl,' he replied, his voice thick with emotion. 'I had to find out if you had married someone else.' He reached for her hand and saw there was no ring on her finger. 'Thank God, thank God,' he said with relief. 'I was so afraid you would have married another man.'

'Pietro, you are the only man I will ever love,' she said. 'But there is another man – Cousin Angelo. My parents want me to marry him.'

Pietro felt the room spinning round and put his hand on the kitchen table to steady himself. Domenica – marrying someone else! How could she!

'No. No, Domenica. Don't do it. *Please*, I beg you.'

She stroked his head and pulled it down to her breast. 'I won't marry him, Pietro, I promise. But you will have to speak to my father and tell him you are going to marry me. When you went away he didn't believe you would come back for me.'

She continued stroking his head, soothing him as she felt his hot breath searing through the thin material of her bodice.

'You said we would marry. Before you went to England, you said we would marry one day. When will that be, Pietro?'

He looked up at her and then because he had to be evasive turned away. 'We will marry soon. Soon, Domenica,' he said. 'One, maybe two years.'

'Two years!' She was horrified. 'I will be twenty-two by then! An old lady!'

'Twenty-two isn't old,' jested Pietro.

'Yes, it is,' she persisted. 'My Mamma had four children by then! What am I going to say to my father? He wants me out of this house, I know. An unmarried daughter of marriageable age is an embarrassment to the whole family. You must know that. I bet your sister will be married before she's twenty-two!'

'I must tell you something, Domenica. When I went to England I thought I could save lots of money very quickly and bring you over as my wife. But it takes longer to save up enough money to do that. Maybe one more year, maybe two, like I said. I promise you I will come back for you. And we will marry in Fizzano and then go to England. I promise.'

Domenica had calmed down by this time. She saw that it was hopeless to have expected Pietro to sweep her off her feet and off to England straight away, much as she would have loved that to happen.

'Just one thing, Pietro, if we are going to do that. Please, please speak to my father!' she begged. 'If you tell him we are engaged to be married, he will let me stay here and not pester me to marry Angelo.'

'That is what we will do,' agreed Pietro. 'We will become officially engaged. I will speak to your father tonight when he comes in from the fields.'


It was an awkward meeting with Tito Soretti. It was obvious he did not trust Pietro as far as he could spit an olive stone. He believed that once he was engaged to his daughter he would disappear back to England never to be heard of again. And then his daughter would be in an even worse position than before. What a disgrace if his daughter was left almost at the altar, so to speak, by this young man!

But after they had a long, heated, discussion, Tito reluctantly agreed to let Domenica become engaged to Pietro.

'But she will wait no more than two years for you,' he

warned.

The good news for Tito was that he would have a little more time to save up the money for the wedding. To a man with six daughters this was like an albatross round his neck – and it would hang there for many years to come, until the youngest one was finally off his hands.

After the meeting with Domenica's father was concluded satisfactorily, Pietro walked to his parents' house in the darkness of the moonless night.

A short way along the route he heard footsteps hurrying behind him. Several footsteps. In the dark he could just make out the shadowy figures of three men running in his direction. A sudden fear gripped him and he started to run, tripping on the rough surface of the unmade road.

The men caught up with him, one of them grabbing him round the neck in an armlock. The others stood in front of him blocking his path.

'Pietro Falgoni?' one asked, menacingly.

'Yes,' he replied, almost choking.

The man loosened his grip but there was no escape for Pietro as the three men stood tightly round him forming an impenetrable circle. Their faces were close up to his.

'We are the Soretti boys,' said one of them. 'Domenica's brothers.'

Pietro immediately relaxed. He laughed with relief. He thought he was going to be robbed – instead it was just his future brothers-in-law playing a little prank on him.

'Hey, boys, you gave me a fright just then!'

The threatening faces stared back at him, unsmiling.

'Are you going to marry our sister?' asked one of them.

'Yes, I am.'

'When do you marry her? This week? Next week?'

Pietro laughed at the absurd suggestion. 'Of course not! I'm going back to England in three days' time.'

The biggest of the three brothers, the one who had grabbed him by the neck, now pulled Pietro's arm up his back making him scream with pain.

'We think you should marry our sister *now*. You have kept her waiting many, many years. People are talking about her because she is unmarried. You have brought dishonour on our family.'

'No, no ..' he protested.

'And we think you have dishonoured our sister,' said one of the other brothers, a thick-set, powerfully-built youth. '*Really* dishonoured her!'

'I haven't .. I haven't ..'

'We want to know, is our sister still pure? Or did you defile her?'

'No …' he replied, 'I mean yes, she is still pure. I have never touched her, I promise.' Pietro was almost lifted off his feet by the arm-breaking grip and was very relieved when Domenica's brother loosened his vice-like hold on him.

'Then when will you marry her? We want to know when our sister is to be married?'

'In one, maybe two years,' he replied hesitantly, knowing this news was going to go down badly with these thugs. 'But we are engaged to be married,' he added hastily. 'It is official. Ask your father.'

The boys grunted and to Pietro's relief seemed to accept the explanation. They were about to walk away from him when the big one grabbed him by the neck again and to his horror Pietro saw the glint of a blade.

'If you don't come back and marry our sister in two years' time, we will kill you. We will cut your throat.'

'Yes, we will cut your throat,' repeated another brother.

'And don't think just because you are in England you can run away from us,' threatened another.

'We know where you are.'

'Yes, we have an uncle in Manchester, Uncle Mario.'

'And he knows where you live.'

As if the threat needed to be made any stronger than it already was, the thick-set youth pushed his face right up to Pietro's, snarling:

'And if *we* don't cut your throat, Uncle Mario will.'

# Chapter 5

The Baileys moved into their new house on a beautiful May morning. The bells were ringing in the nearby parish church as their horse-drawn carriage passed down the lane to Northenden.

Archibald and Elizabeth had four sons and one daughter; but three of the four Bailey boys no longer lived at home. So it was just Mr and Mrs Bailey, their son John, daughter Ellen and a handful of servants who made the move from the house in the centre of Manchester to the countryside. Archibald was hoping that the opulence of their new surroundings would help them settle in without too much upheaval or upset – particularly to Mrs Bailey's delicate constitution.

They approached their new home with the air of adventurers conquering new territory. Bailey's Mount was looking magnificent with its pristine stonework and fresh coats of paint. Surrounded by gardens, fields, and an orchard – and by ample supplies of fresh, clean air – their new family home in its country environment could hardly have been more of a contrast to the one they had left behind, now solely to be used as a town house, in the soot-laden centre of Manchester.

Standing respectfully outside, awaiting their arrival, was the staff of Bailey's Mount – the cook, the housemaid, the kitchen maid, the scullery maid and the gardener. The other employee, the coachman, was driving the carriage containing the family and their personal luggage.

Archibald proudly ushered his family into their new home and took great pleasure in showing them around the finished article, pointing out all the special features he'd personally suggested to the architect.

'All individually designed,' he said, leading the small group from one room to another, 'especially this room... the billiard-room. Just the thing to impress my friends from the Cotton Exchange, don't you think, Mother?'

'Yes, dear, very nice,' said a weary Mrs Bailey.

'Father, I think we need a sundial in the garden,' said Ellen, a few days' later, as the family were enjoying their first celebratory dinner in Bailey's Mount seated round the newly-acquired rosewood dining table.

'Ellen, pass the mint sauce to your brother,' instructed Mrs Bailey, enjoying being mistress of such a grand house.

'This is really excellent lamb,' said John, eating his food with appreciative delicacy – a delicacy that his father did not possess. But then unlike any of his four sons, Archibald had not had the benefit of an expensive public school education.

'Yes, it's a grand bit of meat is this, Mother,' said Archibald, rolling the succulent flesh round his mouth. 'You may be interested to know I had lamb when dining with a business colleague only yesterday. Not as good as this, mind. But it was not a bad price. Let me tell you,' he said, waving a silver-plated fork around in the air, 'we had lamb, green peas, an octave of port and cream cheese

– all for two-and-a-penny, including the waiter's fee of a penny! What do you think of that!' He had that intense look in his eye that always came when he was discussing his favourite subject… money.

'Father, you haven't answered my question,' persisted Ellen. 'I want to know if we can have a stone sundial in the garden. I don't want to hear about how much your dinner cost!'

Elizabeth gasped at the impudence of her daughter. But she knew by now that Ellen could get away with murder as far as her father was concerned.

'A sundial?' he questioned, forcing another roast potato into his already full mouth. 'What's wrong with that gold watch I bought you for your twenty-first birthday?'

'I don't want a sundial to tell the time!' persisted Ellen. 'A sundial is a thing of beauty, a living work of art. And when the sun shines, yes, you can tell the time. But that's not its main purpose.'

'Aye, *when* the sun shines,' stressed Archibald. 'When the sun can get through the Manchester smog.'

'Ah,' chipped in John, 'Now that we've moved out into the country, I'm sure we'll find the sun shines a lot more often here than it does in the centre of town.' 'You see, Father it is a good idea,' persisted Ellen. 'Mr Pietro Falgoni has drawn me the kind of design I would like. He says it will look good in the centre of the lawn.'

'Well, of course he did,' snorted Archibald. 'Anything to get more brass out of me. Those Italians have done very nicely from my patronage and they're just trying to spin it out a bit longer.'

'You must admit,' intervened John, 'that the Italian workmen have made a superb job of the stonework and the decorative stucco. They've brought the Renaissance to Manchester, wouldn't you agree?'

John Bailey, a delicate-looking individual, was a teacher of divinity. He was thirty-three and unmarried. He had spent many months, along with Ellen, supervising the work on the house, making sure that everything was done correctly and to their father's specification.

'I suppose if you want a sundial you must have one,' said Archibald, smiling indulgently at his daughter. 'But get it at a good price. And for heaven's sake don't order any more of those statues. It's like the British Museum out there.' He pointed his fork in the general direction of the garden.

'And another thing,' he added, 'Don't let that Falgoni chappie give you any more of those painted ladies. I don't feel happy having one of them in my house. It looks suspiciously like a Popish church madonna to me.'

'It's not a madonna,' said Ellen hastily. 'It's a painted figurine. It was made by Mr Luciano Falgoni and is a very special Italian *object d'art*. Mr Falgoni junior gave it to me when I went round their workshop in Ancoats choosing statuary for the garden. You must remember me telling you.'

'It still looks like a madonna to me,' muttered Archibald.

If it wasn't for the fact that it would upset his daughter greatly he would have insisted weeks ago that the wretched thing be thrown in the bin. As it was, the figurine was placed in a well-hidden corner of the hall. Hopefully, one day the maid would knock it over while she was doing the dusting.

'Did you say you had been to Ancoats, dear?' Elizabeth asked her daughter, a curl of distaste affecting her upper lip. 'It really isn't a very nice place for a young lady to go to alone.'

'I wasn't *alone*, I was with Mr Falgoni,' replied Ellen with irritation

'Even so, dear, Ancoats is full of all sorts of undesirables so I've heard. Fallen women and the like.' Mrs Bailey wrinkled her nose as if there was a bad smell underneath it.

'Ancoats is where Father has two of his mills, so it can't be all that dreadful,' Ellen snapped back.

'Oh, it's alright for mill girls to be there,' said Archibald. 'And Italians. Lots of Italians live there. All those organ grinders and their monkeys.' He paused for a moment. 'Yes, I see what you mean, Mother. It's not a very suitable place for our Ellen to be hanging about.'

'I wasn't *hanging about* in Ancoats, Father! I was with Mr Falgoni at his work yard. How else am I to see samples of the kind of stone and the designs he does?' replied Ellen swiftly.

'That's as may be, my dear,' replied her father, helping himself to a glass of port. 'But in future you are not to go there unless accompanied by myself or one of your brothers.'

The blood rose in Ellen's pale face, turning her skin a mottled red.

'Then how am I to get my sundial and anything else I need from Mr Falgoni?' she said crossly. Ellen looked as if she was on the point of bursting into tears at the thought of not getting her own way.

'I sometimes think, Ellen dear,' said her mother, 'that you are far too highly strung for your own good.'

Ellen turned her head away and stared out of the window. She didn't trust herself to speak. If she said anything at this moment it would be something really rude to her mother and she knew she would regret it afterwards. But she was seething! What did her mother know about emotions and feelings and sensuality ... and love?

There now, she had admitted it to herself. Love. She only had to think of Pietro Falgoni and her insides turned to jelly. Whenever she was in his presence she was torn between admiring him from afar – and wanting to stand as close to him as decency allowed, breathing in his male perfume, a heady combination of scented hair-oil and fresh sweat.

The months Pietro had spent working on Bailey's Mount had been like heaven on earth for Ellen. She dreaded the day the work would be finished and she would see the young Italian no more. That is why she kept making excuses to order more garden statues – a couple of lions for the front entrance and her latest whim, a stone sundial. She just couldn't bear the thought of never seeing him again.

Unbidden, tears sprung to her eyes.

'You said I could have a sundial!' she said petulantly to her father. 'You *promised*. Just now you did. I'm perfectly safe going to Ancoats on my own. Do you think I'm a baby? I'm twenty-one!'

'There, there,' said her father. 'Don't take on so, Ellen. You shall have your sundial. John will go with you to order it. I could send a lad round from the mill with a written order but I don't suppose any of those foreign chappies read English. Now,' he said decisively, 'let's hear no more about it.'

Mrs Bailey, a look of partial triumph on her face, took the opportunity to change the conversation to a subject that was more to her liking.

'I hear that Neville and Lucy are thinking of going to the Great Exhibition in London next week in Hyde Park.' Neville was the Baileys' eldest son, who worked with his father in the cotton trade. He and Lucy had been married for five years. 'I've heard it's wonderful and that Mr Paxton's glass house is exquisite.'

'It's called the Crystal Palace, Mother,' informed John. 'It's even bigger than St Paul's Cathedral, or so they say. A building of light and air and iron.'

'And glass! presumably,' interjected Archibald who found the concept of a fancy glass building a complete waste of money. But then it was the idea of Queen Victoria's husband Prince Albert, another foreigner, so what could you expect?

Ellen, appeared to forget Pietro and the sundial for one moment.

'I think it sounds wonderful, too. I'd love to go to London to see it before it closes. Not so much for the glasshouse but for all the wonderful things inside it!'

'I've read that there are over one hundred thousand exhibits from all over the world,' John said. 'American grand pianos, Indian silks, steam engines, Italian marble statues… and even the Koh-I-Noor diamond!'

An admiring gasp went round the table. But it was not the Koh-I-Noor diamond that had so impressed Ellen. It was the mention of Italian marble statues. Perhaps Pietro Falguni had supplied one or two of those works of art? And even if he hadn't he was bound to be very interested in seeing works by his fellow countrymen.

'I simply *must* go to the Exhibition,' announced Ellen. 'I will write to Samuel and Margaret,' she said, referring to her brother and sister-in-law, 'and I shall tell them I will be coming to stay with them in London for a few days.'

'*Ask*, dear,' corrected her mother, 'not tell. It's rude just to tell people, even relatives, that you are going to stay with them'

Ignoring her mother completely, Ellen continued. 'I will go down on the train from Manchester. It only takes nine hours. Yes,' she determined, 'I will write to Samuel directly.'

# Chapter 6

The return rail ticket to London cost fourteen shillings and twopence. The train was crowded with hordes of people taking advantage of the specially-priced 'trip' tickets to Hyde Park for the Exhibition. Among them were Ellen Bailey and Pietro Falgoni.

Pietro was delighted to be going on this exciting trip especially as it had come out of the blue. He had of course heard all about the Great Exhibition which had opened two months previously. Father Whitaker who had already visited it told him all about it. He was particularly keen to describe to Pietro the crucifixes and the marble statues. Marble, he told Pietro, so pure and white it must have come from Carrara without a doubt. The statues were made by Italians, he said, and he urged Pietro to go to London and see the Exhibition before it closed in October.

Pietro could hardly believe his luck when the chance came two days later in the form of Miss Ellen Bailey. She and her brother had come to his workshop to choose a sundial. Well, Miss Ellen did the choosing. Mr John Bailey seemed more interested in trying out his few words of Italian on the boys working in the yard outside.

It was after she had placed the order for the sundial that she mentioned the Exhibition.

'I believe there are many wonderful Italian works of

art,' she said, 'Sculpture and all kinds of statuary.' She was standing very close to him and looking up into his eyes in a strange way.

'Yes,' replied Pietro, 'I heard that too. From Father Whitaker. He said I should go down and see it. My uncle however is not very interested in going.'

'Why don't you come with us?' suggested Ellen. 'We're going in September, my mother and I. We're taking the train from Manchester and we will stay with my brother. You could stay at an inn nearby, then all three of us could go round the Exhibition together.'

Pietro was taken aback at the suggestion. 'Your mother would not want me coming along with you I'm sure. She will want to be alone with her daughter.'

'She would love you to come along,' insisted Ellen. 'You could be our guide for the Italian works of art. It would be like having Michelangelo on hand, so to speak!' She smiled her most winning smile and the love-light that shone from her eyes made her almost beautiful.

Pietro was tempted, very tempted. Not by Ellen ... the love-light did not penetrate that deeply into his soul. He was tempted by the opportunity of going to the Exhibition. And if Luciano grumbled about him going he could say he'd combine the trip with a spot of business, offering to visit Clerkenwell and see some of the Italians that Luciano did business with.

When he met Ellen at the railway station on the day they were travelling to London he was surprised to see that she was alone. Mrs Bailey was nowhere to be seen.

'My mother is unwell,' explained Ellen. 'She has a migraine ... *emicrania*,' she said, utilising her newly-acquired language, having started Italian lessons six months previously.

'I'm sorry,' said Pietro, genuinely. 'Is your mother well enough to be left on her own? Perhaps you should have stayed with her?'

'She's not that bad,' replied Ellen airily as they joined the throng of people on the platform. 'The maid is there to look after her. So there's really no need to worry.'

No need to worry, indeed. There was no migraine. Mrs Bailey had never been coming to London to the Exhibition with Ellen in the first place. It was all part of Ellen's elaborate plot to spend time alone with Pietro so obsessed had she become with him.

Her mother believed that Ellen was travelling to London with a girlfriend who was staying in London with her own brother just as Ellen was staying with Samuel. The whole story had been concocted in order to get Pietro to come to the Exhibition with her. She did not wish to appear brazen by asking him to accompany her on her own. That would be most improper. But if it turned out that her mother was indisposed and unable to come along – well that was just bad luck, wasn't it?

Ellen and Pietro managed to get window seats in a carriage that was not as crowded as some of the others. Pietro lifted their overnight bags onto the luggage rack and then settled himself into the seat facing Ellen.

The long train journey passed all too quickly for Ellen who took the opportunity of practising her Italian on Pietro. Pietro, for his part, was flattered by the attention he was being given by this young English lady. He was also very impressed by her Italian. She was the first English woman he had spoken to in Italian. Most of the women he came across in the course of his work or the mill girls in Ancoats seemed to take delight in mocking his attempts at English.

'Speak-a di Engleesh,' they would say, 'Issa verri nice, issa verri good!' Then they'd giggle behind their hands.

But Miss Ellen was different. She had always shown great respect for him and his workmen, appreciating the talent and skill that went into creating the stonework and the modelling of the stucco. She was not a beautiful woman but he believed she had a kind nature.

When the train reached London in the early evening her brother, Samuel, had sent his carriage to meet her. Pietro was dropped off at a nearby hostelry with the arrangement that the carriage would pick him up early next morning and take him and Ellen and her sister-in-law Margaret to Hyde Park. Samuel and his wife had been living in London since he had become a director of the newly-formed London and North Western Railway Company.

It was a pleasantly warm September morning when Ellen, Margaret and Pietro could be seen making their way through Hyde Park and into the Crystal Palace. They were accompanied by crowds of others, many of whom – like Ellen and Pietro – had taken advantage of the special railway-excursion arrangements and the reduced entrance fees – from five shillings to one shilling on four days in the week. This had guaranteed the popular appeal of the Exhibition. Many thousands of working people and country folk who had never travelled in a train before found their way to it.

As Ellen, Margaret and Pietro walked towards the glorious glass structure, Ellen was became ecstatic and cried with admiration, 'This is the most gorgeous sight ever to come before my eyes!'

Her words infected Pietro with their enthusiasm.

'*Magnifico*!' he rejoined.

Even Margaret, not a woman who allowed herself to become over-excited in public, let out a small cry of, 'Dazzling, simply dazzling!'

At the entrance to the Crystal Palace – and representing Courage and Power – was an enormous statue of Richard Coeur de Lion and a mountainous block of coal from one of the Duke of Devonshire's mines.

They walked along the impressive nave towards a fountain with a huge elm tree behind it and started to look at the imposing items on show. Sculpture, jewellery, pottery and fancy furniture were exhibited everywhere around them, together with many odd inventions. They saw a very useful walking-stick for a doctor, 'As long as he did not do too much walking,' noted Ellen examining the object. 'It contains test-tubes and an enema'.

A beautifully-sculpted statue, taking pride of place in the centre of the American section, caught Pietro's eye and he steered the two women in that direction. The sad, submissive face of the carved naked woman, her wrists in chains, struck Pietro as a truly great work of art.

'*Che bella, che bella*!' proclaimed Pietro as he yearned to reach out and touch the statue and feel the smooth marble under his hands.

As Britain was now in the Machine Age it was inevitable that examples of the brand-new machinery should dominate the Exhibition. The two women and Pietro had to compete with crowds of smock-wearing farmers who were monopolising the stands, examining and admiring all the new farm implements.

Then they spied a freezing machine ('Imagine being able to make your own ice!' exclaimed Ellen), and a lady's mechanical writing desk which was constructed in such a manner as to enable the person to write either in a sitting or standing position. One machine that particularly interested Margaret was described as a 'servant's bed'. It had a clockwork mechanism in one leg which made the bed collapse in the early morning, dropping the servant on the floor.

'Samuel and I could do with several of those,' she remarked, 'Our maids seem incapable of getting out of bed before six in the morning.'

Ellen, Margaret and Pietro took in as much of the Great Exhibition as they could in one day.

The next day Margaret was not feeling up to trudging round again and so just Ellen and Pietro spent another few admiring hours at the Crystal Palace before catching the early afternoon train from London to Manchester.

The return journey was longer and more tedious than the journey down. There were delays on the line making the journey nearer to ten and a half hours than nine.

Knowing she would be arriving late in Manchester, Ellen's parents were not expecting her home in Northenden that evening. She had arranged to stay the night in the Bailey's town house where they still employed a couple of servants to keep the place aired and cleaned. Archibald believed it would be sensible to shut down most of the rooms, keeping one or two bedrooms and a sitting room in operation in case any member of the family needed to stay in town after a night at the theatre or a late business meeting.

Ellen's mother and father were under the mistaken impression that this 'girlfriend' who had supposedly accompanied Ellen to London would also be spending the night at the town house.

It was almost eleven at night when the train steamed into Manchester.

'I will get a carriage to take you to your house,' said Pietro as they stepped off the train.

'I would very much appreciate it if you would stay the night at the house, Mr Falgoni,' said Ellen, a look of vulnerability crossing her face. 'Even though there are servants in the house they are below stairs and I do so hate being alone in that big empty building. There are always plenty of rooms made up in case my father needs to stay the night in town.' She could also have added, 'Or in case my brother Neville needs to entertain one of his floosies'.

Pietro was unconcerned. He was quite happy to go the extra mile home to Ancoats but equally happy to stay the night in a grand town house. The way Ellen had asked him not to leave her on her own appealed to his protective manly nature.

And so, foolishly, he stayed.


What followed could almost be blamed on the large bunch of sweet peas the maid had bought in Market Street earlier that day. Or more precisely, on the honey bee that had crawled inside.

Back at the Bailey's Manchester residence the maid set about arranging her fragrant purchase in a vase to be placed on the hall table. Shuffling the long stems, she made a primitive attempt at flower arranging and carried the heavy crystal vase from the scullery to the hall, placing it on the lacy mat covering the highly-polished table. All this activity woke the sleepy bee which rose up and flew directly into the maid's face.

With a scream and a great fluttering of hands the maid ran back into the scullery slamming the door behind her. The bee, just as startled and frightened as the maid, took off in a upwardly direction not stopping until it reached the sanctuary of a large, white 'flower' … a large, white, pillow-shaped 'flower' upon which it landed and crawled underneath.

Several hours later Ellen entered the bedroom and placed her candle on the washstand. The maid had drawn the heavy brocade curtains leaving a small gap through which the moonlight streamed into the room.

Ellen undressed and put on her nightdress. She sat at the end of the bed and unpinned her hair which fell down her back, long and straight and mousy-coloured. She brushed, counting to one hundred as she had done every night since she was a child. But this night she kept losing count, her thoughts far away. Well not too far away. They were on the person in the room adjacent to hers where Pietro Falgoni was also preparing for bed.

This day, this beautiful summer's day, was the happiest of Ellen's life. She had not wanted it to end, so wonderful had it been. That was why she had persuaded Pietro to stay at the house instead of returning to his own home only a short distance away. Pretending she was afraid of being alone had meant Ellen had to swallow a little of her pride. She was a very independent young woman. But it had been worth it. That small sacrifice in self-esteem had gained her more time in the company of the man she loved.

They had dined together on a delicious cold collation prepared by the cook and had talked into the early hours about the wonderful sights they had seen and experiences they had shared at the Great Exhibition.

And now it was all over. She brushed and brushed till her scalp tingled as she plotted new ways of engineering further encounters with Pietro Falgoni. In her head she knew it was hopeless. They were from such different worlds – how could their families ever be united? But in her heart she knew that all things were possible. Why, only this week her father related the story of a local aristocrat – the Earl of Stamford no less – who had recently married a woman who rode bareback in a circus. It was a scandal said her father. Ellen and her mother nodded in agreement but inside Ellen's breast her spirit gave a thrilling leap.

If a landed earl could marry a circus rider, could not a cotton baron's daughter marry an Italian stonemason?

Laying down the brush she separated her hair and began to plait it for the night. A warm glimmer of hope fluttered in her heart like the candle flame that still burned brightly reflecting its glow in the looking-glass.

She moved across and snuffed it out. By the light of the moon she pulled back the sheets and slipped into bed, her dreams of Pietro starting the moment her head hit the pillow.


Pietro in his room across the corridor was likewise climbing into bed. He had never slept in such a luxurious room before. Everything about it was top quality, the very best that money could buy.

He was glad he had been persuaded to stay the night. It meant putting the reality of life in Ancoats behind him for one more night. It was unfair he realised to compare this luxurious room with the one he shared with his cousin Nello at Signora Palomba's. Nevertheless that was what he was doing. And the comparisons served to make him even more determined than ever to succeed in Manchester, to earn as much as he could so that he too could enjoy a lifestyle such as the Baileys.

He vowed that one day he and Domenica – and the children they would have – would become wealthy citizens in a town where all things seemed possible.

His resolve was strengthened even more as he slipped between the fine cotton sheets. He would continue to save his money. That meant no more expensive excursions to London to see exciting exhibitions, no more wasting his hard-earned cash on dirty little whores. Soon he would have enough to bring Domenica to England. And then with the help and comfort of a good wife he would realise his dreams. He would become a *padrone* like his uncle and bring young Italian craftsmen over to work for him in his own business ventures. There were so many opportunities, so much to strive for, so much to gain. And it was all within his grasp.

Just then, just at the moment when he was about to snuff out his candle, he heard a scream. A woman's scream. So loud and so bloodcurdling... and so close.

He ran out into the corridor dressed only in his nightgown, taking his candle with him. The screaming was coming from Miss Ellen's bedroom.

Without a thought he rushed in.

'*Che cosa?*' he called out, lapsing into his native tongue. 'What is the matter?' he asked, seeing the frightened face of the girl in the bed. 'Has somebody hurt you?' he persisted when she continued to cry out in pain.

'Something has bitten me or stung me … on my back,' she said fearfully. 'I think it's still here in the bed.'

She was sitting huddled on top of the bedclothes, reaching round in a vain attempt to find the source of her agony.

'*Momento*,' said Pietro, putting his candle down on the washstand and going over to the stricken young woman.

In seconds he had found the culprit. A small bee still attached by its sting was clinging to Ellen's nightdress.

'It's a bee,' he said, 'I see it now.' He flicked the offending creature off Ellen's back leaving the sting still attached to her body.

'It still hurts,' said Ellen, who was regaining her composure now she knew it was only a humble bee that had attacked her and not some exotic, deadly-poisonous insect or snake.

'That is because the sting is left behind,' said Pietro. 'The bee will die but the sting is still putting in poison.' He knew what he had to do. He had done it many times before on the farm at home.

'Take off your nightdress and I will suck out the poison,' he instructed, adding, 'I will turn my back.'

Ellen slipped her nightdress over her head and held it modestly in front of her.

'Ready,' she said, turning her back to him, face burning, heart racing.

The sting had come away with the nightdress but by feeling gently with his fingers Pietro located the swollen area of the punctured skin. Putting his mouth over the site he sucked out the poison and spat it on the floor. He did this for several minutes until he was sure he had removed most of the poison. He then stroked the hurt place with his fingertips gently soothing and caressing her skin.

It gave Ellen a very strange feeling. The pain had gone but another pain took its place, the pain of longing. She did not want him to stop touching her, stroking her with his hands so firm yet gentle. The feel of his mouth on her bare flesh inflamed her senses and sent a tingling through her entire body making her nipples harden like tight rosebuds. All these sensations flooded her mind and took control of her body.

'There might be a little more poison in there I think,' she said softly just when she imagined he might be taking his hands away.

'I will make sure,' said Pietro, placing his mouth on her fragrant skin once more.

This time as he touched her he felt her relax and lean towards him. Her body was no longer tense with pain, no longer frightened he might hurt her.

As he gently sucked and licked the place with his tongue he heard a small moan escape her lips.

'There is still pain?' he asked anxiously.

'No,' she whispered, 'no pain.' She breathed in deeply and turned to face him. In the soft half-light he saw her lips were parted, her eyes languid. Her perfume was warm and enticing as it entered his nostrils.

'I had better go now,' he said huskily, making no attempt to move from the bed.

She was still looking at him, still holding her nightdress in front of her. Then she moved her arms a fraction letting the garment drop. She was naked, pearly white in the moonlight. Her breasts were small, but round and firm like succulent little fruits.

Pietro stared at her body, transfixed.

She put her arms up to him, inviting him, demanding him. The blood that had rushed to his head – and other parts of his body – beat a rhythm that could not be ignored.

He responded as if to a primitive drumbeat, taking her in his arms and crushing her to him. His mind was taken over completely by the urges and needs of his body.

Tearing off his night-clothes he lay on top of her, parting her thighs.

'*Cara mia*' he murmured as she yielded to him.

She gasped as he entered her. Even then, when he knew he should stop, he could not … his mind was beyond reason, beyond the point of no return.

Even so, he sensed something was different about this woman. All the others he'd made love to had been whores. This one was a virgin. His first virgin.

The realisation of what he had done struck him the moment he had achieved orgasm. Until then he had no other thought than that of his own pleasure, his own need. When he withdrew from her he saw in the moonlight the blood on the white sheet. He knew he had done a most terrible thing.

'I'm so sorry, I'm so sorry,' he kept repeating, fear taking a grip of his soul. 'How could I do such a thing?'

Ellen on the other hand was happy, joyously so.

'Don't worry, Pietro,' she said comfortingly, taking his head between her breasts. 'We could not help ourselves. We could not help it. It was God's wish that we should do this thing.'

# Chapter 7

The day Queen Victoria and Prince Albert came to Manchester was the most brilliant day the town ever beheld.

Loyal crowds greeted the royal couple … schoolchildren and workpeople lined the route all dressed in their Sunday best. The royal party, accompanied by the mayor in his fine robes, drove through the Manchester streets to the Exchange where the main ceremonies of the day were to take place.

The Exchange was a fine building in the centre of the business area of town where hard-nosed textile merchants and manufacturers did the deals that filled their pockets – and the coffers of the town – with silver and gold.

Archibald Bailey through his membership of the Exchange had managed to secure tickets, priced at one pound each, for members of his family. They had arrived early, a good two hours before the royal party was due. While they were waiting in the Exchange – to be known from that day forth as the 'Royal' Exchange – the town clerk gave them all a lecture on royal etiquette.

'Quite unnecessary,' grumbled Archibald. 'Just because we're in trade he seems to think we're all ignorant peasants! Let's get on with it!'

But before the Baileys could even get a glimpse of the Queen, Ellen passed out slithering to the floor and causing a commotion in the crowded hall. Her parents took her outside for air, missing the royal arrival and the civic ceremony.

'I did *so* want to hear the Queen speak,' complained Mrs Bailey. 'I've been told she has such a sweet, clear voice.'

'Do be quiet, woman,' scolded Archibald, sounding equally annoyed at having missed the highlight of the royal visit. 'Whatever's the matter, Ellen?' he asked crossly.

'I don't know,' she said. 'I think it must have been the crowds.'

'I've never known you to faint before,' said her mother with thinly disguised irritation.

'You were always fainting I seem to recall, Mother,' said Archibald, determined to blame someone for his spoiled day. 'She probably inherited the weakness from you.'

'I only ever fainted when I was with child,' protested Mrs Bailey. 'I never fainted like Ellen. For no reason at all.'

Her mother's words 'with child' rang accusingly in Ellen's ears. It had been ten weeks since she had lost her virginity to Pietro Falgoni and in all that time she had not had her 'female monthlies'.

Later that day, after she had rested for a while at the town house, Ellen felt well enough to join in the continuing celebrations of the royal visit.

She and her parents walked around town admiring the illuminations and joining in with the good-natured crowd as they all pressed on towards Piccadilly. The warehouses in the area were lit up by gaslight. Multicoloured illuminations were reflected in the pond in front of the Infirmary, its three fountains making a dazzling display. As they strolled past the pond Archibald couldn't resist telling her a story his old mother used to tell him. She pretended to hear it for the first time.

'Your grandmother,' he said to Ellen, 'could remember them using the ducking stool in this very pond to punish fallen women. What do you think about that!' Because there were ladies present he did not used the word 'prostitute'.

The words 'fallen women' stung Ellen like nettles on bare skin. A picture formed in her mind − a picture of herself strapped into a chair at the end of a long pole as she was ducked for her sinful behaviour.

During the evening they went down into King Street to admire the luminescent lamps outside the shops and Town Hall. In St Ann's Square, there was a magnificent triumphal arch. It was here that Ellen spied Pietro with a group of his Italian friends.

Pushing her way through the merry crowd she went up to him, smiling.

'Hello, Pietro. What a wonderful day this is for Manchester.'

'Oh, hello Miss Ellen. Yes, it is a wonderful day, *magnifico!*' he said, laughing and waving his arms in the air.

Ellen got the distinct impression that Pietro and his friends had been drinking alcohol, and quite a lot of it. She had not seen him since the trip to the Crystal Palace… and the memorable night of the bee sting.

Although she knew she loved him with all her heart, and imagined he must also love her (why else would a man make love to a woman?), she had not seen him face-to-face since then. She had left messages for him at his workshop, mainly about the sundial and other stonework needed for the garden. Something, however, had stopped her from writing to him about more personal matters.

Even though she had no regrets about losing her virginity to Pietro – he was, after all, the man she loved – she felt slightly discomforted about the whole episode. She kept wishing the intimacy had not happened quite so soon. She wished the relationship could have been given time for these things to develop in the usual way – through courtship, engagement… and marriage.

However, 'intimacy' had happened, and now she had a very worrying feeling that things had raced ahead all too quickly. She had – for several weeks – acknowledged a nagging suspicion that she might be pregnant. The lack of her monthly bleed, the morning sickness… and now the fainting earlier that day had only served to confirm what she already feared. The sooner she discussed the matter with Pietro, the better. Now, of course, was not the ideal time particularly as he seemed to be drunk.

'Miss Ellen,' he said jovially, 'My friends and I have just been in the King's Head and I am very happy.'

All his friends found this very funny and spoke loudly in Italian to each other. Ellen found their accents hard to follow and couldn't understand what they were saying.

'Pietro,' she said, raising her voice over the noise and hilarity of the crowd, who were now lustily singing 'God Save the Queen' for the umpteenth time, 'I must speak to you urgently. Tomorrow. I'll see you tomorrow. *Domani*,' she added in Italian for emphasis and clarity.

'*Si, domani*,' he replied. 'I see you tomorrow, Miss Ellen.' One of his friends made a remark in Italian and the whole group guffawed loudly. She had the uncomfortable feeling she was being discussed by these young men in an inappropriate way. The sooner she left their company the better.

Squeezing her way back through the crowd she joined her parents. Archibald slipped an arm around his wife and his daughter and, infected by the great happiness of the occasion, all three walked homewards.

# Chapter 8

Early next morning Ellen took the omnibus into town. Before going to see Pietro she called in to see a doctor. A polished brass plate was attached to the door of his smart consulting rooms in St John Street.

No, she hadn't an appointment, she told the lady who answered the door. Yes, she would wait.

One hour later, she was on her way to Ancoats, her pregnancy confirmed.

Pietro had no recollection of Ellen telling him that she needed to see him urgently. In fact he had little recollection of any of the events of the previous day. All he had to remember the royal visit by was a splitting headache that had kept him in bed three hours longer than usual.

Instead of taking the train to Bowdon that morning, to meet an architect and discuss a new job, he would have to travel the twelve miles on the afternoon train. He hoped the architect would still be willing to use him and his workers and hadn't taken umbrage and decided to give the work to someone else. Pietro felt pretty confident this job would go to him even if he was late for the first appointment. He knew, and so did the architect, that his Italian workmen were the best stoneworkers money could buy. He also knew that the cotton barons wanted only the best for their fancy new country houses.

Pietro had refused a large cooked midday meal at Signora Palomba's and settled instead for a ham and salami sandwich on thick, crusty Italian bread.

He was walking along the dusty street towards the railway station when he saw a familiar figure stepping out of a carriage at the street corner near his workshop. It was Miss Ellen.

He hadn't seen her, he thought, since the night of the bee sting and all that had followed. A vague recollection of seeing her yesterday flashed into his mind but as most of the events of that day were in an alcoholic haze he could not be sure of anything that had taken place.

Seeing her hurrying towards his workshop, all the guilt and embarrassment connected with that evening in July came flooding back to him. In the following weeks he had tried to push it to the back of his mind and had succeeded in doing so. He considered himself very fortunate that she had not pursued him or accused him or sent her brothers or father after him.

He felt relieved as the weeks went by believing he had got away with the dreadful thing he had done – deflowering the daughter of one of the richest, most powerful men in Manchester. The experience had taught him a salutary lesson. From now on he would keep his sexual urges well under control and wait until he was married to Domenica – which he was sure would not be many months away.

He was looking forward to going to Italy in three days' time, to order more stone and marble and also to bring back more Italian apprentices. The stonemasonry business was getting snowed under with work – which was good news as far as the money was concerned – but they needed to expand and bring in more workers. If they couldn't deliver the goods they would soon start to lose orders.

There had been a great upsurge in commissions from the Bowdon area where many gentlemen's houses were being built on plots of land recently made available by Lord Stamford. Word had got round that the Falgonis were the best for stonework, and architects and builders were beating a path to their workshop in Ancoats.

Another reason he was looking forward to going to Italy in a few days was, of course, to see Domenica. And this time he was going to fix a date for their wedding. He had enough money saved to rent some rooms in a house in Ancoats close to other Italian families. It wouldn't be a grand house like the ones he'd worked on in Manchester and the surrounding countryside but it would be a start, their first home, and it would mean they could at least be together. One day he planned to build Domenica and himself a beautiful house – but that was all in the future. For now he was just dreaming of taking her in his arms and loving her. It was a dream that occupied his thoughts day and night.

As Ellen hurried along the street Pietro ran after her.

'Miss Ellen,' he called, 'did you come to see me?'

She turned on hearing his voice. 'Oh Pietro,' she gushed, 'I'm so glad to see you! So glad!'

As he reached her he saw to his horror that her smile had faded and her lips were beginning to tremble. She covered her face with her gloved hands and began to sob. Automatically he put his arm around her in a comforting gesture.

'Are you unwell, Miss Ellen?' he asked. 'Let us go

and sit down outside Signora Palomba's shop over there.'

They walked the few yards to Signora Palomba's Italian provisions shop which, during the summer and early autumn, sported a couple of tables and half a dozen chairs on the pavement outside in an attempt to encourage customers to sit down and order an ice cream or a coffee. Usually the chairs were occupied by Italian men who, after drinking in The Red Dragon, continued their heated discussions and socialising without purchasing anything.

As Pietro and Ellen sat down, Signora Palomba came to the table to see if they wanted anything. Signora Palomba was bursting to know what was going on but instead just asked in her best English: 'Would the young lady like a *gelato,* Pietro? Issa warma day and she mighta find it nice-a fresh.'

'I don't know,' replied Pietro. 'Would you like an ice cream, Miss Ellen. Italian ice cream is very good.'

Ellen said nothing, but just shook her head, dabbing at her eyes with a lacy handkerchief.

'Issa the young lady not well?' enquired Signora Palomba, unable to keep her curiosity to herself.

Pietro realised it had been a bad idea to bring Ellen here to sit down and it was now going to take ages to find out what her problem was – especially if his landlady insisted on hovering round their table constantly asking questions. He had a train to catch if he was going to get to Bowdon before the architect lost patience with him. And he had a lot of other business to deal with before he caught the boat to Italy.

He gave Signora Palomba a penetrating look and she took the hint, leaving the two young people together but watching them from a discreet distance behind the counter of her well-stocked shop.

'Now you can tell me what you are crying about,' said Pietro gently, a dreaded feeling coming over him as he began to wonder if perhaps he was responsible for her tears.

'Oh, Pietro, it's so terrible,' she whispered. 'I don't know how to tell you.' She sniffed a little and then gave him that direct gaze he found so unsettling. 'I'm going to have a baby!'

She blinked and paused before adding: 'Your baby.'

Pietro felt as if he'd been struck a heavy blow with a blunt instrument.

'A baby? Are you sure?' he gasped in disbelief.

She nodded. 'I've just been to see a doctor in town and he has confirmed I am pregnant.'

Pietro was shocked. Deeply shocked. What on earth was he going to do? Thoughts raced through his mind. Pregnant! He had made a girl pregnant! It made no difference who she was, or whether he loved her, his choices were very limited. In fact, they were limited to one. He would have to marry her. Of course. Yes, that is what he was going to have to do. He spoke his thoughts out loud.

'We will get married,' he said haltingly, hoping against hope this was all a joke she was playing on him and that any second now she would burst out laughing.

'Yes,' she said with relief. Then a warm smile came to her face. 'We will get married. Oh, Pietro, how happy that would make me! I love you so much. And I know you love me. It will all work out in the end, I know it will.'

She relaxed against the back of the cane chair and began to pull off her gloves, finger by finger.

Pietro however had taken on the tense, anxious mannerisms that had belonged to Ellen when she had arrived ten minutes previously.

Married to Ellen? What on earth was he talking about? How could he possibly marry this woman when he was already engaged to Domenica, the girl he had loved since he was sixteen? The girl he was planning to bring over to Manchester as his bride in a few months' time?

He did not speak for several minutes but just stared down at his hands, gripping the edges of the small wooden table.

Ellen was chattering on about plans for the future and he wasn't listening. He couldn't take in a word she was saying. All he could think of was Domenica and the beautiful look on her face when he had said they were to be engaged. What was he going to tell Domenica now? More to the point, what was he going to tell her terrifying father and rough brothers? If he didn't marry Domenica he was a dead man – they'd made that much clear to him.

'Pietro,' said Ellen, 'You're not listening to me.'

He looked up, leaving his daydreams behind. Back to reality.

'You are having my baby ...' he stated quietly in an incredulous voice, not wanting to speak loud enough to be heard by Signora Palomba, listening behind the open door of her shop.

'Yes,' she said, almost proudly now. 'I'm having your baby. And I'm so happy about it – because now it means we will be married. My father will not wish to prevent our marriage once he learns of my condition. If I know him he will want it to happen very quickly to stop any scandal or gossip circulating round the Exchange!'

She was talking away so excitedly and so quickly that

Pietro was finding it hard to keep up with her.

'Your father? Your father knows?' This was one more item of concern for Pietro.

'He doesn't know yet,' replied Ellen, 'You will have to come and see him tomorrow or the day after and talk to him about it. You will have to ask him if you can marry me. In English the phrase is "I would like your daughter's hand in marriage". Can you remember that, Pietro? He will be very impressed if you do it the right way. He's a bit of a grumpy old thing but his bark is worse than his bite.'

'Bite?' said Pietro with concern. 'Your father will bite me?'

'No, no, no! Not *bite* you! That is only an English expression.' Ellen was now back to her old, confident self.

'Come the day after tomorrow,' she ordered, 'in the evening when he's had a chance to relax a little after business. Tonight I'll soften him up a bit, prepare him for the fact that his only daughter is going to get married. I won't tell him I'm pregnant of course, not until we've got everything settled. Then we can just mention it so that he will let us get married as quickly as possible.'

'The day after tomorrow?' said Pietro, suddenly realising the implication of everything. 'That's when I leave for Liverpool. And then I sail for Italy and will be away for several weeks choosing stone and marble and employing workers …'

He was going to add 'and seeing the girl to whom I'm engaged to be married'. He gulped. My God, what was he going to do? What a mess he was in.

Ellen's face hardened. 'You can't!' she said petulantly, 'You can't leave for Italy! You have to stay here with me and speak to my father!'

He thought she was going to start crying again so he reached over and took her hand in an effort to calm her.

'It will be all right,' he said. 'I'll think of something.'

'How can you say it will be all right if you're going to Italy! You can't go away! Not now. You just can't!' Ellen's voice took on a strident tone.

Signora Palomba, alerted by Ellen's raised voice, could control her curiosity no longer. Poking her head round the shop door she asked 'Everything orla right, Miss?'

'Yes, thank you,' said Ellen, dismissively, not even turning to look at Signora Palomba. Lowering her voice she said to Pietro, almost threateningly:

'If you don't see my father the day after tomorrow, there will be trouble. I thought you loved me, I thought you wanted to marry me. I'm having *your* baby, remember. Your little Italian baby. So don't tell me you're too busy to see my father.'

'I will see your father,' he said without emotion, not knowing how he was going to order his affairs. All he knew was, he had to see Archibald Bailey the day after tomorrow, come hell or high water.

# Chapter 9

Two weeks later in Fizzano, Nello knocked at the Sorettis' front door. This was the part of the trip he was most dreading. This was the moment he would have to tell Domenica – and her father and brothers – that his cousin, Pietro, was no longer able to honour his promise of marriage. There was a distinct possibility he was putting his own life at risk.

'You will have to go and tell her, Nello,' Pietro had told him – almost begged him – the day Ellen Bailey had turned up in Ancoats.

Nello thought it was sweet, very sweet, to have his bossy cousin throwing himself at his feet so to speak, asking for his help. Ever since their uncle Luciano had forced the two young men to work together, to eat, drink and even share a room together, Nello had harboured a seething resentment towards Pietro. Luciano had promised Nello *he* would be the boss when they got to England. Then the moment their uncle had got them settled in Ancoats and taken their passports 'for safe keeping', he discovered that Pietro had been told the same story and been promised the same deal.

Splitting the responsibilities, making each cousin a boss, had fooled no-one. Everyone knew that Pietro had been given the most important job as the boss of the stonemasons. And didn't he let them know it!

So when Pietro came to him ashen-faced telling of his terrible predicament – that he had made a baby with a rich Englishman's daughter and he could no longer marry Domenica – Nello was finally able to take his revenge and exact a big price for the favour he was asked to do.

'Please go to Italy in my place and buy the stone and marble,' said Pietro. 'And please tell Domenica I can no longer marry her because …'

'Because you are marrying an English girl,' butted in Nello.

'No, no, don't tell her that! Her brothers will murder me.'

Nello gloated when he recalled the fear in Pietro's eyes.

'Tell her I am dead,' implored Pietro. 'Tell her she must marry someone else because I am dead. And make sure her brothers know that I am dead. Will you do that for me, Nello?'

Nello spun out his reply as long as he could, making Pietro sweat a little more. Of course Nello was not going to miss the chance of going to Italy in his place. He had asked Luciano many, many times why Pietro was sent to order more materials and not him. Nello objected to Pietro or Luciano always choosing the terrazzo tiles that his workers used. Did they think he was incapable of striking a good deal? What did they think he was? Did they think he was *stupido*?

'If I do this for you, Pietro,' said Nello, striking a bargain with a man who was in no position to negotiate, 'I want a promise from you that you will cut me in on all your new contracts.'

'On my stonework and sculpture?' said Pietro, incredulously. 'You want a share of my wages?'

Nello nodded, a lazy smile playing on his lips.

'Fifty per cent.'

'Fifty per cent! You must be crazy,' stormed Pietro. 'You think I'm going to shell out half of my earnings to you – for doing nothing! What do you think I am?'

'I think you're a man in a very bad position,' replied Nello. 'What is the point of keeping all your earnings if you are going to have your throat cut by the Sorettis?'

Pietro cursed. Nello knew that his cousin must be regretting having told him about the incident in Fizzano. Nello had him over a barrel.

'Ten per cent,' he offered. Nello shook his head smugly.

'You'll have to do better than that, Pietro,' he said, running his fingers across his neck in a throat-cutting gesture.

'Twenty per cent. That's my final offer.' Pietro said in despair. 'If you won't go to Italy for me, I'll ask Luciano.'

Seeing his opportunity slipping away, Nello stopped twisting the knife.

'Twenty five per cent and we've got a deal,' he said.

'Done. You bastard.'

The two cousins shook hands, sealing the contract.


Nello had enjoyed the early part of the trip, strutting up and down the offices of the quarry managers, striking what he considered to be good deals for the stone and marble. He also enjoyed exacting a few sweeteners for himself, being entertained at the quarry owners' expense and taking his pick of the ladies of the night that were offered to him as inducements.

He ordered some of the stone from his father's quarry for family reasons, making sure his father got a good price for it. Nello had to pay over the odds but this was family – how could he be expected to beat down his own father on price? And now, here he was, quaking in his boots outside the Sorettis' house, about to fulfil the part of the bargain he'd been most dreading.

What if the Soretti boys didn't believe the story about his cousin having died? What if they suspected the truth – that their sister had been dishonoured by a broken engagement? That the whole family had been dishonoured? What if they took it out on him?

'Hello,' said the young woman as she opened the door and saw a smartly-dressed young man standing outside. 'Can I help you, sir?'

'Domenica?' asked Nello nervously, making a great effort to avert his eyes from her beautiful breasts.

'Yes.'

'I am Nello Falgoni. Pietro's cousin.'

Her face softened into a warm, welcoming smile. 'Oh come in, Nello.'

He followed her into a shabby room where a sullen-looking youth was seated at the kitchen table eating a piece of bread and cheese and drinking wine.

'This is Pietro's cousin,' she said to the youth. 'Nello, this is my brother Gino.' The youth grunted, his mouth full of food.

'Please sit down, Nello. Can I get you a drink of water, or some wine?'

He sat down on one of the wooden chairs round the large kitchen table.

'Wine, please, *signorina*.' Nello was going to need a little dutch courage to get him through the next few minutes unscathed.

'So tell me about Pietro,' she said, pouring red wine into a glass tumbler. 'Is he well? Is he coming to see me soon? We are engaged, you know. We are getting married very soon. He wrote me a letter saying he has saved up a lot of money and is coming over to arrange the wedding day.'

She wouldn't stop chattering, she just wouldn't stop talking. On and on and on, about Pietro. Nello was rapidly losing his nerve.

'I have bad news about Pietro,' he eventually managed to say.

His words stopped her in her tracks. She sat down heavily on a chair facing him across the table. All the colour had drained from her face.

'Bad news?' she whispered.

Nello gulped his wine, draining the glass.

'He is dead.'

Domenica gave a small cry and slid off her chair onto the floor in a faint. Gino looked accusingly at Nello.

'Now see what you've done,' he spat out the words, flecks of cheese shooting across the table. 'You've upset my sister with your bad news.'

Nello jumped up and went to Domenica's aid. Gino remained seated, stuffing his mouth with more bread.

He got her back on to the chair and she came round slowly, holding her head in her hands, leaning on the table for support.

'Dead?' she said hoarsely. 'He can't be dead. Pietro, dead?'

'I'm sorry, Domenica,' said Nello, putting a comforting arm around the distressed girl. 'I'm sorry to have to bring you such bad news but he asked me to come and tell you.'

'He *asked* you?' She wiped her tear-stained face and looked up and him, puzzled.

Nello could have bitten off his tongue.

'Just before he died,' he said, moving back to his chair, desperately playing for time while his brain worked overtime. 'He drowned, you see.'

'Drowned?'

'Yes. In the River Irwell. It's a big river that runs through Manchester. We managed to get him out but we were too late and just before he died he said "Go and tell Domenica".'

Nello was beginning to warm to his subject. 'He said "Tell her I love her, but I can't marry her" … that was because he knew he was dying, you see.'

Domenica began to sob.

Encouraged, Nello embellished his story even more.

'It was on the day Queen Victoria came to Manchester, just a few weeks ago. We were standing on a special platform by the river and it collapsed, throwing lots of people into the water.'

'You fell in, too?' asked Gino, interested in hearing the gory details.

'Yes, and I rescued the women and the young children who were floundering about crying piteously for help.' Nello was beginning to enjoy this.

'Pietro, too? Did he rescue others?' asked Domenica between sobs.

'Some. Not as many as I rescued. I am a better swimmer.' Nello was not keen to show Pietro in as good a light as himself but he had to make the story credible.

'And then, exhausted by his effort, he was hit by a large piece of wood on the head, sending him to the bottom of the river.'

'Oh, mercy!' exclaimed Domenica, crossing herself. 'Santa Maria! My poor Pietro!'

'So I dived in and tried to rescue my brave cousin but to no avail. I pulled him to the bank and it was there, on the banks of the Irwell, he breathed his last. A prayer on his lips and his thoughts on you.'

Nello was even beginning to believe the story himself. Tears had sprung to his eyes. Domenica was sobbing. Even Gino stopping chewing and looked as though he had been taken in by the little drama enacted by Nello.


He left the Sorettis' house and walked back along the path to his Uncle Alfonso's farm, feeling very pleased with himself. He was sure they would have no trouble from the Sorettis. He just had to square things with Pietro's parents in case they heard rumours of Pietro's demise. He'd stayed with his aunt and uncle the previous night and had told them the truth – that Pietro had got an English girl into trouble and would have to marry her.

Alfonso and Seraphina had taken Nello's news about their son quite well, all things considered. They had been helped to come to terms with Pietro's sinful behaviour when Nello had told them that the girl in question was the daughter of a rich man. A very, very rich man.

The more Nello thought about this aspect of the situation, the more annoyed and jealous he became. Trust Pietro to fall on his feet! he snarled to himself. What a lucky beggar he was! His cousin would soon become the son-in-law of a rich mill owner. He would without doubt move away from the squalid tenement houses of Ancoats and into an elegant mansion bought by his future wife's father. It was all so unfair.

The measly twenty-five percent of Pietro's future earnings in stonemasonry seemed paltry compared with what his cousin was in line to get once he married that Ellen girl. Alright, so she was plain. Extremely plain – thin and peevish-looking with no breasts to speak of. But who was going to be bothered about that? Weren't all women the same in the dark?

# Chapter 10

Archibald Bailey stood in front of the ornate marble fireplace warming his ample backside. He liked a nice fire and insisted on one being lit most evenings, even on an evening like this with the weather unseasonably warm for early autumn.

He appreciated his home comforts after a hard day's work at the mill or the Exchange. His new house, Bailey's Mount, was everything he wanted it to be. A mansion fit for a cotton king – plenty of spacious rooms, sumptuously appointed, and enough servants to make the running of it smooth and uncomplicated.

He had insisted upon that. He couldn't stand his wife, Elizabeth, nagging on about what a lot of work the new house was going to be. He soon sorted that out by agreeing to her every wish. That soon shut her up.

He gave a little chuckle. Elizabeth would have her work cut out to find something to grumble about – but no doubt she would. Missing out on seeing the Queen at the Exchange had given her days of complaining. Fortunately that could be laid at his daughter's door not his. Women!

At that moment the objects of his thoughts walked in. Both of them, his wife and his daughter.

'Father,' said Ellen, 'I have someone in the hall who would like a word with you.'

Archibald looked up questioningly.

'It's a young man,' said Mrs Bailey, much to Ellen's irritation.

'Let *me* tell him,' said Ellen crossly.

Pietro had arrived just at the moment Mrs Bailey came down the stairs. Ellen had been hoping that this first meeting between Pietro and her father would take place without her mother being present. As it was she was going to have to play it straight down the line having missed the opportunity to soften up her father the previous night as he had stayed in town after working late.

'Will one of you tell me what's going on?' said Archibald.

'Father,' began Ellen nervously, 'there's a young man outside in the hall who wants to ask you something. Something about me.' She gave him a penetrating stare. 'You *know*. Something important.'

Archibald was intrigued. He thought he had got the gist of what Ellen was hinting at. Was some young blade going to ask to marry his daughter? He smiled to himself. Well, we'll see about that. His daughter was twenty-one and of marriageable age. But she was his precious child, his princess. It would have to be a very exceptional young man that won his approval and gained permission to marry Archibald Bailey's only daughter.

'Right my dear,' he said, smiling indulgently. 'Announce the young man.'

Pietro was waiting nervously in the hall, dressed in his smartest suit with his cleanest shirt and most expensive necktie. His boots were polished and his freshly-washed hair was slicked down with scented hair oil.

Ellen came into the hall and beckoned to him. With

shaking limbs he followed her into the Baileys' drawing room. He felt as if he was making a journey to the gallows.

'Father, this is Pietro Falgoni. You have met him already. He is the sculptor in charge of all the stonemasons who have been working on this house,' Ellen announced.

Archibald's disappointment was all too obvious. His face dropped a mile.

'I hope you've not come to pester me for more orders for wretched garden statues,' he said ungraciously. 'We've got far too many as it is.'

Pietro took a deep breath. His mouth was dry. He tried to swallow but there was no spittle in his mouth. Making a great effort to hide his Italian accent he said the words he had rehearsed over and over again.

'Mr Bailey, I would like to ask for the hand of your daughter in marriage.' Pietro felt himself beginning to blush. This was the most awkward meeting of his life. He was made to feel even worse by the aggressive look on the other man's face.

'You what?' said Archibald in a most unfriendly manner.

Pietro wanted to sink through the floor. Was his English really so incomprehensible? He made another attempt at enunciating the words Ellen had ordered him to say.

'Mr Bailey, I would like to ask for the hand...' Before he was able to finish the sentence he was interrupted.

'I heard what you said the first time,' bellowed Archibald. 'I just couldn't believe my ears!'

Turning to his daughter he demanded, 'Ellen, tell me

this is a joke. A joke in very bad taste, I might add. Tell me you aren't serious.'

'I am serious, father. *We* are serious. Pietro and I have fallen in love and want to get married.'

At this news, Mrs Bailey clutched the side of a leather wing chair to stop herself falling over with the shock.

'You're going to marry *him*?' she asked her daughter incredulously. 'A *stonemason*?'

'You may well say that, my dear,' stormed Archibald. 'Our daughter has lost her senses. Marry a stonemason? An *Italian* stonemason? A foreigner! Foreigners are people you employ, you don't *marry* them!'

Ellen decided to turn on the tears.

'Oh, Father,' she blubbed, 'how can you be so cruel! I love Pietro and he loves me.'

'There, there,' said her father, comfortingly. 'I'm sure he does love you, my precious. You're such a lovely girl, who wouldn't love you? I love you. Your mother loves you. We all love you. And I'm sure lots of young men love you. But that's no reason to throw yourself away on some johnny-come-lately who's only interested in your fortune.'

At this offensive remark, Pietro felt the blood rush to his head.

'I am not interested in your daughter's fortune!' he said angrily. 'That is not why I ask to marry her!'

'Don't raise your voice to me, young man,' snarled Archibald menacingly. 'You want to get back to the slums of Italy where you came from. Marry some dusky little wench from over there instead of trying to steal one of our English roses.'

The offensiveness of the insult incensed Pietro even further.

'How canna you say this thing!' he said, his Italian accent becoming more pronounced as his words tumbled over one another in his anger. 'I amma not from de slums. I amma from good family, verra good family. My father, he havva big farm. He havva his own workmen! I no wanna your money.' He beat his chest. 'I, Pietro Falgoni, will getta lots of money, just like you!'

Archibald, fearing a fight might break out in front of the ladies, tried to calm things down.

'Yes, alright, lad. I'm sure you will earn lots of money. But you're still not having my daughter! Is that clear?'

'But I love him!' wailed Ellen, 'I love him!'

Pietro, who felt humiliated and insulted by this fat, rich, old man, could not find the words in English he wished to say, so filled up with emotion was he. Instead, speaking in Italian, he said to Ellen, *'Perché non parlare di nostro bambino?'*

Hearing the young man speaking Italian in front of him only served to reinforce Archibald's dislike of foreigners and all they stood for.

'And that's another thing,' said Archibald, 'You Italians are Catholics aren't you? Papists. Well, if you think I'm having my daughter marring a Catholic you've another think coming.'

This aspect of the situation had not occurred to Ellen. She knew her father had an unreasonable fear and hatred of Catholicism and Catholics … but she had not thought about religion in connection with Pietro. She had known he had done work on a church in Ancoats and at the back of her mind she must have known it was a Catholic church. She also knew from visits to his workshop that the Falgonis sold religious statues. Indeed she had been given one of the small painted statuettes that Pietro called a *figurina*. Her father called it a Popish statue and banished it to a corner in the hall. Even so, until that moment she had not fully realised the implication that marrying an Italian might also mean marrying a Catholic.

'Are you a Catholic, Pietro?' she asked tentatively, crossing her fingers behind her back.

'Yes, I amma Cattolico.'

'See! I told you, Ellen,' said her father triumphantly. 'So marriage is quite out of the question. You don't think I'm prepared to have little Popish grandchildren do you?' The thought was so absurd it made him laugh. 'So that's the end of that! I suggest you leave now, Mr Falgoni.'

Ellen placed herself between the two men.

'It's too late, Father. I'm having a baby.'

Once again her mother grabbed the chair. 'A baby!' she gasped.

This time Mrs Bailey had to sit down as her legs had given way with the shock of what her daughter had just revealed.

Archibald said nothing. The colour rose in his neck, up his chin, over his ears, right to the top of his bald head. Ellen thought he might have a seizure.

For Pietro it was like being in a nightmare. Could it really be true that he was asking for the hand of this plain, petulant girl – and being brutally insulted by a bully of a man for his pains? And all so that he could act in an honourable way. He sighed resignedly.

'It's true,' said Pietro who was now the calmest person in the room . 'That is why I am asking to marry your daughter. We are having a baby. A *bambino*.'

But he wasn't to stay calm for long. Hearing Pietro's words brought Archibald back to reality. He pushed Ellen aside and grabbed Pietro by the lapels, almost lifting him off his feet.

'Don't think you've won, you greasy little fortune hunter! You may have seduced my daughter in order to slide your slimy Italian feet under my table – but that's not how it works in the Bailey household. That's not how it's going to be if I've anything to do with it!'

Pietro found himself being swung round and given a heavy thump between his shoulder blades. He was propelled through the drawing room door and out into the hall. A further push and he was sent sprawling on the hall rug.

Ellen ran after him fearing her father was going to hit him again.

'No, Father don't hurt him I beg you!'

'I'm not going to soil my hands on the beggar. I just want him to leave now. That would be in his best interests. Perhaps you'd convey that message to your ex-boyfriend.'

Pietro scrambled to his feet and made a lunge at the larger man.

'No, Pietro,' said Ellen, fearing a bloody confrontation. 'Do as he says,' she begged.

'I will kill him,' said Pietro putting up his fists, knowing he'd never been so insulted in all his life.

'Just go home,' said Archibald.

'Yes, Pietro,' pleaded Ellen, 'go now and we will talk about this later.'

Pietro stood in the hall, dusty and dishevelled, shaking with anger. He looked from Ellen to her father and back again. Impotent with fury, he realised there was nothing more he could do that evening. He decided he'd better go home to Ancoats and consider his position. Ellen was right. They would talk about it later.

'Orla right!' he yelled after Archibald who had turned his back on him contemptuously. 'I go now, but I come-a back!'

Pietro walked briskly out of the house, down the dark path.

Archibald, a man who couldn't resist having the final word, shouted to Pietro's retreating back, 'Yes, you go now. But you no come-a back!'

Catching a glimpse of the hated statuette he picked it up and flung it with all the force he could muster in Pietro's direction.

'And take your Holy Mary with you!' he yelled.

In the darkness Pietro heard the sound of the figurine shattering into a thousand pieces as it hit the stone path.

# Chapter 11

'So *now* you tell me what all this is about!' stormed Pietro's uncle. 'Only now do I find out why I had to send that idiot Nello to Italy to buy stone instead of you. Only *now* do you come and tell me you've got a girl in trouble. And not just any girl. The daughter of one of my most respected customers. *Now* you tell me!'

'I'm sorry, Luciano, but everything happened so quickly. Things are very complicated.'

Pietro had knocked on his uncle's door the moment he returned to Ancoats after the appalling confrontation with Archibald Bailey. He needed help and advice from Luciano. What he really wanted was to speak to his own father who was always so wise and all-seeing. His Papa would know what to do. But Luciano would have to do instead.

In a few short sentences he told his uncle the whole story, even down to the bee sting. When he'd finished, Luciano was furious. Not at Pietro's stupidity, but at Archibald Bailey's insulting behaviour. He took it personally.

'How dare he!' raged Luciano. 'How dare he speak to an Italian like that. As if you were nothing, a nobody. You were quite right, Pietro, to leave his house with your head held high!' Pietro hadn't told his uncle about being flung out of Bailey's Mount by the scruff of his neck.

'What should I do next?' asked the younger man.

'You must go back and claim what is yours,' decided Luciano. 'She is your woman and she is carrying your child. That child is family. It is yours ... it is ours.' He flung out his arms as if to encompass the whole Italian nation.

Pietro was silent. Luciano was right. He owed it to his unborn child not to be frightened off by Archibald Bailey.

'You love this girl, do you?' enquired Luciano.

Pietro hesitated. 'I don't know. I don't think so. But she is a nice lady and I feel I should marry her.'

'Well, there you are. This is what we will do.' Luciano had a plan. 'You will bring Miss Ellen to live in Ancoats. Signora Palomba has two rooms she is going to let out – the two rooms next to where she makes her ice cream in the basement. I will speak to her and say you will be taking them for your wife and child. Then we will go to Father Whitaker and get the marriage organised. Miss Ellen is over twenty-one I think?' Pietro nodded. 'That is good,' said Luciano. 'She does not need her father's permission to marry. There now! That is all sorted out." He slapped his nephew heartily on the back.

His uncle's confidence made Pietro feel as if the deal had already been done... and that he was as good as married to Ellen Bailey. His heart missed a beat at the thought. It was Domenica he should be marrying – not this rich man's daughter!

'But what about Domenica?' he blurted out, unable to stop himself. 'I love only her.'

Luciano's face became serious. 'For a moment I had completely forgotten about your fiancée. We will have to sort it out with her family, that's for sure. The Sorettis might want to take revenge on you for dishonouring their family.'

'I'm not worried about that,' Pietro said with bravado.

'Well, you should be.'

'She thinks I'm dead. Nello has gone to tell her in person.' He didn't add 'for a price'. The last thing he wanted his uncle to learn was that he was being blackmailed by his cousin. What an even bigger fool that would make him look.

Luciano relaxed. 'That's fine, then. Why should they try and kill a dead man?' He winked at Pietro.

Pietro was enveloped by an overwhelming sadness. 'I can't bear the thought of losing Domenica,' he uttered. 'She is the only woman I have ever loved. And now I've lost her.'

Luciano spoke sternly to his nephew. 'You have made your bed, my dear boy, and now you have to lie on it!'


Pietro went to his room that night torn apart by a mixture of emotions. Marriage to a woman he did not love was a grim prospect... losing his sweet Domenica through his own foolishness was ever harder to imagine. But then so was the idea of losing his child – his own flesh and blood.

He had been brought up to believe that a man always accepts his responsibilities and the biggest responsibility of all was to the family. The unborn baby was now his family and his responsibility. He must forget all that had gone before, forfeit all the hopes he had for a home and children with Domenica. That was all over. Domenica was now in the past.

Father James Whitaker was charmed by the idea of performing a marriage ceremony for Pietro.

He was so pleased this nice young man had found such a respectable girl. One who appeared to come from a really good family. She hadn't spoken as yet but he could tell from her clothing and her demeanour as she sat very still in the vestry of St Agnes's Catholic Church that she wasn't 'common clay'. Her pale face seemed very white in comparison to that of her olive-skinned beau seated next to her.

'When had you in mind for getting married, Pietro?' asked Father Whitaker smiling benignly. 'Next year, perhaps?'

'Next week,' said Pietro, blushing deeply. 'Or at least as quickly as possible.'

'Oh, I see,' said the elderly priest putting the tips of his hands together. 'Is it because of, shall we say, family circumstances?'

'Yes,' Pietro replied, shamefaced.

'Oh, I see,' repeated Whitaker.

Pietro could tell from the disapproving way the priest spoke those three words that he'd let down the old man. Pietro felt humiliated. He lowered his eyes, unable to meet the other man's gaze.

There was a short, embarrassed silence, then Ellen spoke.

'I'm not a Papist,' she said. Her voice steady and assertive. 'Does that make any difference?'

'In a way, it does,' said the priest. 'It means you cannot have a nuptial mass because it will be what we call a "mixed marriage" – a Catholic and a Protestant. You will be married on the side altar of the church. But of course in the eyes of the church, you will still be married.'

Ellen nodded

James Whitaker outlined the marriage arrangements. Banns would have to be read out and the marriage would be performed as quickly as permitted by special licence. 'Under the circumstances,' he added.

How sad, thought Father Whitaker, that this nice young couple were 'having to get married'. It was usually the lower class of mill girl who found herself in the family way these days, pondered the priest as he took down their details. Not a well-spoken young lady like this Miss Bailey. And Pietro – one of his most regular altar servers! That he, of all people, should get a girl into trouble. Whitaker shook his head sadly as the young couple left the church vestry.

'This is Signora Palomba,' said Pietro, introducing Ellen to his landlady.

The Signora had already met Ellen a few days before when she was sobbing her eyes out at one of her street tables. It was all clear now. The girl was having a baby. No wonder she had been sobbing her eyes out. If one of Signora Palomba's daughters ever found herself in that shameful position she'd give her something to sob about!

When Luciano and Pietro had spoken to her about renting the basement room for the boy and his new wife, Signora Palomba guessed something was afoot.

'Your girl is coming over from Italy?' she had enquired. No, answered Pietro. It wasn't an Italian girl he was marrying.

'A mill girl, perhaps?' probed the curious Signora.

'In a way,' replied Pietro coolly, annoyed by this

cross-examination. 'Her father owns several.'

Signora Palomba drew in her breath. 'And she is coming to live here? In my humble basement? What does her rich father think about that?'

'Signora,' said Luciano gently, 'can we count on your discretion?'

The woman nodded, her eyes out on stalks.

'My nephew, Pietro, has found himself in a little difficulty.' Luciano put a paternal arm around the embarrassed Pietro. 'The young lady is having his baby and her father is not too happy about it.'

Signora Palomba bit her tongue to stop herself giving Pietro a lesson on pre-marital purity.

'So what we thought, Signora,' continued Luciano diplomatically, 'is that the young couple could rent your basement and when the baby comes along you will be there to lend a motherly hand. It will be an *Italian* baby, after all.' He gave a hearty laugh.

It was all settled. Pietro just had to get Ellen accustomed to the idea. He hoped desperately that she'd agree because that was all he could afford, especially with a baby on the way.


And here they were, straight after speaking to Father Whitaker, looking into the disapproving eyes of Signora Palomba. She beckoned the young couple to follow her.

Ellen stepped gingerly down the stairs leading to the basement apartment under the Palombas' shop.

The stone floor was clean and the walls freshly white-washed. The only day-light came from a small window high up on the wall located at street level. In the centre of the room was a threadbare rug and a wooden gate-leg table. The table was covered with an Italian lace cloth.

'That's very pretty,' said Ellen trying to find something good in the whole grim set-up.

In the other room was a rickety-looking bed with a patchwork quilt and another thread-bare rug on the floor.

Ellen walked around the humble apartment as if in a trance. She knew the moment she'd stepped inside she had no intention of living there. It was the most awful experience of her life discovering how the majority of ordinary Manchester people lived. Her father would have a fit if he could see her now.

After the terrible confrontation with Pietro, Archibald had told Ellen she must never see that 'gigolo' again.

'But I'm going to marry him, Father,' she had insisted, bravely standing her ground.

'If you do, young lady, you're on your own. Not a penny can you expect to get from me. Let him keep you in the manner to which you've become accustomed. I'd like to see him try.'

Ellen was determined to prove her father wrong. When Pietro, instead of taking flight after the row with Archibald, had persisted in his attempt to marry her, Ellen was convinced he loved her. What need had she of money? She and Pietro would live on love alone!

As she climbed the stairs back from the basement into the Palombas' shop, she was beginning to change her mind. She couldn't *possibly* live in a basement in Ancoats! And she couldn't stand to have that appalling Signora Palomba as her landlady, sticking her nose into everything she did. Taking Italian lessons was one thing. Being surrounded by a whole immigrant colony babbling away in the language was a totally different matter! She wanted to marry Pietro, yes. But she didn't want to live

120

anywhere near his compatriots in Ancoats.

'So, Ellen,' said Signora Palomba taking a matriarchal stance, 'I am like a Mamma to Pietro. I cook him nice Italian food. I teach you how to make-a pasta and orla good things. You can call me Mamma Palomba.'

Ellen thought she was going to throw up. First the prospect of living in a basement in Ancoats, then the idea of that bossy woman lording it over her. It was all too much.

Ellen sobbed and pleaded. She whined and wailed. She ranted and raged. All to no avail. Her father was unmoved.

'Ellen, if you insist on marrying that despicable young man, and in a Popish church no less, you get no sympathy from me. And not a penny comes your way either. And you know why? Any money you have, any house I buy you, any possessions you have – as far as married women's property is concerned – it will all belong to him. That's the law of the land. Now, if you think I'm going to hand over my hard-earned brass to that scoundrel, think again.'

'But what about the baby? I can't live here as an unmarried mother. You're not suggesting that are you?' Her bloodshot eyes, red and puffy from crying were turned helplessly in her father's direction.

He softened. 'Nay, lass. I'll not have shame and disgrace brought upon thee. I have it all worked out if only you'll listen to me. In a few months' time nobody will be any the wiser and everything will be all right.'

'Oh, Papa,' sobbed Ellen.

Archibald opened his arms and his daughter ran to him for comfort, just like she did when she was a little girl.

# Chapter 12

Domenica had taken the news of Pietro's death very badly. Every day she wept for hours on end, hardly noticing anything that was going on around her. If she helped her mother with the housework she did so like a zombie, just going through the motions as if in a trance.

And then, one Sunday after Mass, Domenica heard some very disturbing news.

She was kneeling at the back of the church, having lit a candle, and was saying prayers for the repose of Pietro's soul. One of her friends came and knelt beside her.

'I've got some news for you,' whispered the girl in hushed tones. 'My sister's best friend is Francesca Falgoni and she told my sister something in confidence. She said that her brother is *not* dead. He is having to marry some girl in England because they are having a baby! But keep it to yourself, Domenica. If your brothers find out, Pietro will be as good as dead.'

'Pietro is alive?' Domenica exclaimed. She could hardly believe her ears.

'Shhh!' warned her friend. 'It's a secret. You mustn't tell anyone, particularly your brothers. Francesca will blame my sister if any of this gets out.'

'But you don't know what you're saying!' hissed Domenica. 'His cousin Nello came over and told me so himself. Told me that Pietro had drowned rescuing women and children. He died a hero. His cousin told me!'

'And you think that he would tell you the truth do you, Domenica?' murmured her friend. 'Do you think he would tell you that his cousin has to marry another girl, an English girl, because he got her pregnant? Do you really think any of the Falgonis would dare say that to your family?'

'But... it can't be,' gasped Domenica, the blood rushing to her head making it spin round like a top. 'I don't believe it. I *won't* believe it!'

But deep inside, she did believe it.

She went up to the candle she had lit for Pietro and snuffed it out.


The conversation with her girlfriend changed Domenica's life. No longer did she pine after Pietro Falgoni, believing him dead, weeping for the man she loved, her heart breaking from the sadness. Instead she hardened herself to accept the truth. Pietro was alive and living in England! He had deceived her, lied to her. And while she was waiting patiently keeping herself pure for him, what was he doing? Having a baby with an English girl, that's what he was doing!

That same day, Domenica told her father she would marry Cousin Angelo. The wedding took place eight weeks later, in the village church in Fizzano. The same church where Pietro Falgoni had sung as a choir boy and where she had imagined that one day she would marry him.

Domenica scrubbed the front step of the little house which was in one of the poorer streets of Fizzano.

Since her marriage to Angelo she had enjoyed playing the role of housewife, cleaning and polishing and washing to her heart's content, making the few small rooms comprising their rented house into a warm and welcoming home. She loved everything about being a housewife. In particular she loved cooking delicious meals for her new husband when he came in from the fields, and she rose early each morning to catch the best bargains in the market.

She and Angelo had been married for almost half a year.

After she'd scrubbed the step to her satisfaction she closed the door and made her way to the next street and her parents' overcrowded house.

Until she had babies of her own it was natural that Domenica should lend a helping hand to her mother, particularly as her mother was pregnant once again.

'Mamma,' said Domenica as she helped her with the heavy items of washing, 'How do you have a baby?'

'All too easily!' exclaimed her mother resignedly, sitting down heavily on a hard kitchen chair. 'Your father only has to hang his trousers on the end of the bed and I get pregnant!'

Domenica had never heard her mother talk in such an intimate way before. The woman chortled to see her daughter's reaction which she mistook for prudery. Rubbing the swollen, itching varicose veins that riddled her heavy legs, she laughed.

'It's all right, Domenica. You're married now. We can talk about these things, woman to woman. We both know what men are like in that direction, don't we?' She gave a coarse laugh.

'But *how* do you have a baby?' persisted Domenica, uncomprehending.

'Oh, don't worry about all that,' replied her mother, dismissively. 'When the time comes you'll know what to do. I'll be there to help you, and the midwife too. I'll get you a nice strong piece of linen for you to hang on to, tied to the bedstead, for when the pain gets bad. And when you think the agony will go on for eternity your little *bambino* will slip out into the world!'

Maria Soretti looked knowingly at her daughter. 'Domenica, are you telling me you're having a baby? It's about time, I suppose. You and Angelo have been married six months, already. I'm sure I got pregnant with you the day I got married! Certainly your father was keen enough on our wedding night to ensure several times over I was no longer a virgin! No doubt Angelo was the same. But that's Sicilian men for you. Ah, now I've made you blush!'

Domenica was certainly blushing. But not because her mother was speaking so crudely about Angelo's bedroom antics – because there hadn't *been* any bedroom antics. Domenica was blushing because she felt foolish. Foolish and ignorant.

'Mamma,' she said, dropping her eyes to the floor, 'I don't know what you are talking about. When I ask "How do you have a baby?" I don't mean how do you give birth. I mean how do you get pregnant? Does a man *really* just hang his trousers on the end of the bed?'

Her mother began to laugh, believing Domenica was having her on. No newly-married woman needed these things spelling out to her by her mother, surely? A girl found out those things on her wedding night. But

126

something in the way Domenica lifted her head and looked into her mother's eyes made her recognise the truth.

Her mother spoke quietly and gently.

'Domenica, are you telling me you are still a virgin?'

'I think so, but I don't really know what it means,' said the girl desperately.

'Domenica, has Angelo ever … done anything to you? Anything in bed?'

'He lies down next to me,' replied Domenica. 'That's all.'

'He doesn't *do* anything? Anything with his you-know-what? Like the animals in the field? You *must* know what I'm talking about!'

Domenica shook her head. She felt so alone, so miserable, so embarrassed.


Later that same evening, when Domenica and Angelo had finished their meal, her father and brothers turned up on their doorstep.

As she opened the door they pushed past her and confronted a very startled Angelo who was just draining the last dregs of wine from his goblet. He was taken aback by the posse standing before him, fixing him with accusing stares.

'What is it, Tito?' he asked in surprise.

Without looking at his daughter, Tito ordered her out of the room. 'This is men's work,' he barked.

Through the thin walls of the bedroom she could hear every word that was said.

'You have shamed my daughter,' accused Tito. 'You have brought shame on the whole family.'

She could hear the sound of a chair crashing onto the stone floor.

'What right have you to come barging into my house and accuse me of anything!' retorted Angelo, raising his voice.

'That's just it,' she heard her brother Gino sneer. 'We're accusing you of nothing. Because you haven't *done* anything. That's the whole point!'

'What's the matter with you? I don't know what you are talking about,' protested Angelo.

'We are talking about my daughter, Domenica,' said Tito. 'She tells us she is still a virgin! And you two have been married six months! You insult my daughter, you insult my whole family. Is she so unattractive you can't bear to act like a husband with her? What kind of man are you, Angelo? Answer me that!'

Domenica listened in horror from the bedroom. Hot tears of shame ran down her cheeks. She had no idea her mother would tell her father such intimate things! There was silence from the kitchen and she strained to hear what was going on. Then she heard a choking sound. They were hurting Angelo! She ran out of the bedroom in order to defend her husband.

But instead of finding her father and brothers attacking Angelo she was greeted by the humiliating spectacle of her husband crying like a baby.

He gave her a look of pure hatred. 'You told them. You bitch!'

'Of course she told us,' said her father. 'We would have found out in any event when you didn't give her any babies. Don't you think people would ask questions?'

Then her father did a terrible thing. He grabbed her by the arm and thrust her towards Angelo. Her brothers, also, pushed her towards him.

'Do the decent thing, Angelo,' he said. 'Make her a proper woman or the whole village will think there is something wrong with my daughter. Do it tonight. Make her a woman.'

Instead of holding her, Angelo pushed her back towards her father and brothers. To her shame, Domenica found she was being used like a shuttlecock, shoved backwards and forwards between the men.

'Take her back then, if you feel like that,' shouted Angelo.

'She's yours now! Not ours!'

'I don't want the bitch. Take her back.'

'You'd better not say that again,' threatened Gino, picking up a meat cleaver from the kitchen table and holding it to Angelo's throat.

He knew the game was up. With sweat pouring down his face, Angelo spoke in panic, the words tumbling out in a rush.

'All right, all right! It's my fault! My fault! I admit it. Put the knife down. Don't cut me! Don't kill me!'

When the situation had calmed down, Angelo told them that as a result of his terrible wounds he was impotent. He imagined that being married to someone as lovely as Domenica would change matters, giving him back his manhood. Sadly, that had not been the case. So his wife was still a virgin and he felt terrible shame because of that.

As Angelo confessed the tension eased. Tito even managed to be magnanimous. At least he could now hold his head up high as no blame could be laid at his doorstep.

'You were a freedom-fighter, Angelo,' said Tito.

'That is very honourable and your wounds are honourable wounds. So we don't blame you now that we know the truth. We feel no dishonour on our family, no disgrace. Domenica will stay with you as your wife and nobody will say a word about this outside the family.' He looked at his boys meaningfully. 'Is that clear? We keep this to ourselves.'

Pointing at Domenica he ordered: 'If anyone asks you why you are not having any babies you will say that the Lord hasn't blessed you yet and that you are praying every day. Everything will be fine, you'll see.'

It was all very well for her father to say that. But everything was not fine. From that day onwards her marriage was in tatters.

'I will never forgive you for telling your family about this,' said Angelo to her when her father and brothers had left. 'Never. And I will never forget what you have done to my pride. Now, slut, clear up this mess and scrub the kitchen floor before you come to bed. And in future I want more wine in the evenings. Much more. And if you don't do what I tell you this is what you'll get.' He hit her brutally across the face with the back of his hand, cutting her lip.

'And even if you do what I say, you'll still get this.' He struck an even harder blow to the other side of her face, knocking her to the ground.

Stepping over her, he went into the bedroom.

# Chapter 13

Pietro hadn't seen Ellen since the day he brought her to Ancoats to arrange the wedding and show her where they'd be living. The next day he received a hand-delivered message from her, written in rather bad Italian, telling him she was not pregnant. It had been a false alarm. There was no baby and therefore there would be no wedding. He was not, she instructed, ever to contact her again.

It was this final sentence that Pietro found so humiliating.

'She insults me! What does she think I am? A gigolo, going round pestering her for favours? Is that what she thinks!' Pietro was incensed. Luciano and Signora Palomba were in the shop when a messenger boy delivered the letter and witnessed his anger and embarrassment.

*Mamma mia*! He hadn't wanted to marry the girl in the first place! But he was a man of honour and was going to do the decent thing. What right had she to turn him down in such an offensive manner?

'Those Baileys! Who do they think they are?' He spat venomously out of the corner of his mouth. 'A curse on them!'

'Hey, not so fast,' said his uncle with false jollity. 'We've had a lot of business out of them, remember? So

let them keep their women and we'll keep their gold!'
He slapped Pietro on the back.

A few weeks later, Pietro heard that Domenica had married her second cousin, Angelo. Now there was no chance he could ever make her his! The devastating news had come via Mario Soretti who lived in Ancoats, an uncle of Domenica's who had travelled from Italy with Luciano thirty years previously.

'He asked me to give you the message,' said Luciano.

'*Dio mio*!' exclaimed Pietro, the implication of how he'd got the news striking him like a thunderbolt. 'This means Mario Soretti knows I am alive!' The colour drained from his face. 'I have dishonoured their family name by breaking off the engagement to Domenica. Now he will have to kill me!'

'No, he won't,' said Luciano calmly and with confidence. 'I've sorted it out with Mario. There will be no vendetta in Ancoats. He and I have come to an arrangement so you need have no fear.'

Pietro closed his eyes in relief... An arrangement. He knew exactly what kind of arrangement his uncle meant. Luciano would have to pay blood money to Mario Soretti.

The moment Signora Palomba had realised Pietro would not be marrying that toffee-nosed English girl she set to work. She sent word to her sister in Como to bring her daughters back to England after nearly seven years in Italy. Now was the ideal time for her elder daughter to capture the heart of her favourite lodger! And once Marietta was living with her again, Signora Palomba lost no time in engineering little meetings between the two young people. Under her own roof of course. She wasn't going to risk her daughter's reputation by allowing her to be seen outside the house with a young man on her own. That would never do. A red-blooded young Italian male could hardly be blamed if a girl was foolish enough to act in a scandalous way. That Bailey girl had brought her shame upon herself, considered the Signora. And even though it was a false alarm about the baby, that young lady had behaved like a street girl. Thank goodness Italian girls are brought up with a stricter moral code, she shuddered. Stricter than those English and Irish girls.

Very soon Signora Palomba had manoeuvred the young couple into marriage.

As for Pietro, after the emotionally bruising experiences of recent months, the simple kindness of his landlady's daughter helped him regain his self-confidence and pride. He had quickly been won over by Marietta's charms – mainly because she bore a striking resemblance to Domenica. Marietta was a plumper, dumpier version. But her smile was heart-stopping in its likeness to Domenica's as she looked at him shyly from under thick black lashes.

The church of St Agnes's where the marriage would take place was only a few streets away from where they lived. Everyone who had gathered at the Palombas' house that morning set out on foot in a procession behind the bride and her tall, handsome brother.

Marietta's younger sister Angelina wore her best traditional costume with a long skirt and apron, red waistcoat and a white blouse, her beautiful black hair covered with a white headscarf. She was so proud walking behind her big sister on her special day. 'The most important day of her life,' sighed Angelina, longing to be a bride herself.

The church was filling up with wedding guests and on-lookers. Signora Palomba had promised her daughter 'a real Italian wedding, just like back home'. Marietta's wedding, she promised, would be one of the most lavish Ancoats had ever seen. Everybody connected with the families had been invited. A few close relatives had even managed to travel from Italy. The Signora's sister, Anna who had looked after the girls ever since their father had died, had come over. And to Pietro's great pride and joy his brother, the priest Antonio, had arrived from Rome and would marry them.

The guest list was long and what they lacked in family they made up for in compatriots. Virtually every Italian in Manchester had been invited, as well as close neighbours and valued customers from Palomba's shop. Luciano, the senior Falgoni family representative and the bride's godfather, had invited several business contacts including some from Clerkenwell, London's 'Little Italy'.

Even the feared Mario Soretti had been asked. ('Alright, so we don't like him – but we must invite him because he's a compatriot. If we don't invite him, he'll be offended,' reasoned Luciano.)

'She's taking a long time, perhaps she's changed her mind,' said Nello mischievously to Pietro. He might be the best man but Nello wasn't beneath needling a nervous groom on his wedding day. The love-hate relationship between the two cousins continued unabated.

'All brides are late, that's the tradition,' snapped

Pietro.

'I was just thinking, you know, with your luck with women.'

'A best man is supposed to give support to the groom not get him worried.'

He was getting fed up with Nello and his constant harping on about women, comparing his success rate to Pietro's.

'I'm only your best man because your brother Giovanni couldn't come over. I know when I'm second best,' Nello said sulkily.

So that was what he was annoyed about, thought Pietro.

'And I thought you were in a bad mood because I'm marrying Marietta. I know you are sweet on her!'

Pietro was only joking but Nello went bright red. Before he could respond, Marietta's brother, Luigi, who had been delegated to watch for her arrival gave the signal that the bride and her entourage were now walking up the path to the church.

As the bride and her family entered through the church door, Pietro sneaked a quick glance. He saw Marietta on the arm of her eldest brother, Carlo, her face obscured by a long lace veil. Pietro caught his breath … For a split second he imagined that it was Domenica walking down the aisle as her face drifted towards him from the past.

'Hope you're marrying the right one,' whispered Nello as if he could read his mind.

'Shut up, Nello or you'll be sorry afterwards.' He spoke through clenched teeth as he stepped out into the aisle to greet his bride.

As Pietro slipped the bright band of gold on Marietta's finger and Don Antonio pronounced them man and wife

– the enormity of what he'd just done struck home. He was now a married man, married to a girl he had known for a few short months. A girl whose main claim on his heart was that she looked a little bit like Domenica. Domenica, his true love.

*'Hope you're marrying the right one.'* Nello's words came back to him, but only for a moment.

He looked into Marietta's soft brown eyes and saw the love that reached out towards him. He *would* love Marietta. He would try to love her with all his heart… if only he could forget Domenica.

After the Mass, following tradition the newly-weds had sugared almonds thrown at them outside the church symbolising future prosperity. Dozens of children, appearing it seemed from nowhere, dived to the ground picking them up.

There were shouts of 'Long live the bride!' ringing through the air from the crowd of people who had gathered in the street outside, shouting and clapping as the wedding party made their way on foot to The Red Dragon and the reception.

'Pick up your dress, Marietta,' fussed her mother. 'It will get all filthy round the hem from the dirty streets.'

But Marietta, clinging to the arm of her new husband, was too happy and carefree to worry about a little thing like that. An Italian organ grinder was outside The Red Dragon to greet them with his repertoire of wedding day tunes. His pet monkey caused great hilarity by making a grab at Marietta's veil making her shriek.

In the downstairs rooms of the pub, wine and small salted biscuits and nuts were being served to all the guests on arrival.

The tables were laden with huge quantities of Italian

wine and beautifully decorated with flowers and candles. Signora Palomba had organised the entire function.

Waiters brought round vast platters of tiny pastries filled with mushrooms and tomato, and canapés of large green olives, tiny veal sausages, *crostini* of chicken liver paté and the thinnest slices of Parma ham and stuffed eggs flavoured with anchovy and capers.

After the *antipasti* came the pasta, and then the main course – aromatic roast pork with green beans and potatoes roasted in meat juices and whole cloves of garlic and rosemary. Dessert was Signora Palomba's famous ice cream in three different flavours, raspberry, apricot and vanilla.

The wedding cake was carried in to loud applause.

There was one person, however, who didn't feel like joining in the applause –Nello. Watching Marietta and Pietro ceremoniously cutting the cake, he felt a dagger pierce his heart. She was so lovely, this little round-faced beauty. He truly loved Marietta – but she had never given him any encouragement. It was as though her mind had been poisoned against him. He had been captivated by her the day he got home from work and found her helping in the shop with her younger sister. They had just arrived from Italy. His heart gave a leap when he realised she would be living under the same roof as him. But it was no use. Right from the start Signora Palomba had made it quite clear that Marietta was reserved for Pietro. So there was only one thing for him to do today and that was to get drunk.

The wedding celebrations went on for hours. All through the meal guests proposed toasts to the bride and groom or their parents and godparents, and the chant of '*bacio, bacio, bacio*' went round the room, everyone insisting that the groom should kiss the bride. Then came the dancing to an accordion band.

Signora Palomba looked on proudly as Pietro and Marietta took to the floor. '*Che bella! Che bella!*' she said for the umpteenth time that day.

After most of the guests and revellers had taken their leave, a group of close family and friends set off in procession to install the newly-weds in their new home. This was a rented house next door to Palomba's shop and furnished out of Marietta's generous dowry.

As he lifted his bride over the threshold, Pietro was looking forward to a new life, a new beginning. And even if he was not *in love* with Marietta he was well on the way to loving her. Loving her with his whole body if not his whole heart.

# Chapter 14

It was a supreme irony that at the precise moment Pietro and Marietta consummated their marriage, Pietro and Ellen's son made his entrance into the world.

The midwife let Ellen see him for a moment. A tiny bundle of wrinkled flesh with a shock of black hair. For a second Ellen gazed transfixed into the most beautiful eyes she had ever seen – and the child seemed to gaze back at her.

'Best not to get too attached to the little fellow,' said the midwife, handing him over to the wet-nurse.

But it was too late. Ellen had seen him and had looked into his soul. He was hers and she was his.

For ten days the midwife and the wet-nurse looked after Ellen and the baby in different rooms of the same house. At regular intervals, Ellen could hear the baby's little cries, like the sound of a mewling kitten. Cries that called out to her in the long, sleepless nights. Cries that made her want to rush into the nursery-room down the corridor and snatch him from his crib and hold him to her breast. Oh, how she longed to hold him! But instead of following her instincts she just wept into her pillow.

'Now Miss Ellen, don't be upsetting yourself,' ordered the midwife. 'Just forget about baby. He's not your responsibility now. Your responsibility is to yourself and your good family. You must rest and built up your strength and then you will be well enough to go back home to Manchester.'

Ellen's body was crying out to feed her son. Her breasts, painfully distended and bound up with yards of bandaging, were filling with milk. Milk that had to be 'sent away'.

'Don't be drinking anything, Miss Ellen,' instructed the midwife, moving the carafe out of reach. 'Only tiny sips of water are allowed. The milk will go away of its own accord if baby isn't put to the breast. We can send the milk away much quicker if we cut down on our liquids, can't we?'

*'I don't want to send the milk away!'* Ellen felt like screaming in the woman's shiny, round face. *'I want to feed my baby!'*

But she knew it would have been to no avail.

*'I have it all worked out'*, her father had said. *'In a few months' time, nobody will be any the wiser.'*

She had gone along with his plan because she had little choice, and because she had seen the wisdom of his words. Ellen could no more have married Pietro and lived in Ancoats than gone to the moon. But when she agreed to do what her father had suggested she had no idea that nature would be so cruel. No idea that once the baby was born, how different she would feel about it. She truly believed that when she'd had the baby she could forget all about it and carry on with her life as if nothing had happened.

But the moment she saw that tiny creature, so small, so vulnerable, she knew she would never, ever forget him. She knew that for the rest of her life she would be haunted by that one glimpse of his little face and the sound of his baby cries. It was primitive and primeval. It was torture.

For ten long days and nights she suffered the anguish of knowing that her baby was close by in another room, being fed and cared for by another woman, when every nerve in her body yearned for him.

'You're a lucky girl having had such an easy birth,' said the midwife after the first week, unwrapping the breast bindings. 'Your figure will soon be back to normal.' She squeezed Ellen's breasts one at a time, to check on them. Satisfied the flow of milk had almost dried up, she replaced the bindings. 'Feeding a baby can do such terrible things to your bosoms. That's why all the smart London ladies have a wet-nurse. The discomfort of binding the breast is a small price to pay for being able to wear a *décolleté* gown to society balls, wouldn't you say?'

Ellen felt the bile rise in her throat. She wanted to strike the woman. But somehow all the fight had gone out of her – all her independent spirit had been crushed like a small bird inside a powerful hand... her father's powerful hand.

'This is what we'll do, lass,' he had said the day she realised she could not live an impoverished lifestyle in Ancoats. 'You will go and stay with your brother Samuel in London. They'll look after you. Margaret will be glad of the company as Samuel is always away on railway business. I'll tell your friends and people in Manchester that you're spending some time in London, visiting the theatres and museums and all that kind of thing you ladies like doing so much. You'll have the baby in London. I'll pay for a top-class midwife to look after you and a wet-nurse for the child. The child will be adopted by a childless couple of good standing who will have no

141

idea that the baby is any connection with us. A perfect solution to a tricky little problem. I've had it all worked out for days. I knew you'd never go through with marriage to that particular young man. Just write him a note saying it was a false alarm.'

'Oh, Papa,' sobbed the relieved Ellen. 'Will everything be all right?'

'Yes my little one,' comforted Archibald. 'Trust me. Everything will be all right.'

And for the first few weeks of her stay with Samuel and Margaret everything did seem to be all right. She had been made very welcome in the expensive Mayfair residence of her brother and sister-in-law. It was only when her pregnancy began to be more obvious that she noticed a distinct change in Margaret's attitude towards her. Previously very friendly, she began to act in a strange manner.

'Is there anything the matter, Maggie?' asked Ellen one evening as the two were doing a little needlework together. 'Are you feeling unwell?'

'No,' snapped her sister-in-law. In the embarrassing silence that followed, Maggie stared at Ellen, or rather at her stomach. Then she blurted out:

'You're very lucky having a baby! It's not fair. I want a baby and nothing seems to be happening. It's not fair,' she repeated.

To Ellen's horror, her sister-in-law started to cry. Easing her bulk off the chair she went over to comfort her.

'Oh, Maggie, I'm sure you and Samuel will have a baby soon. Lots of babies.'

The woman shook her head miserably.

'Not according to the doctor. He says I might be...

barren.' She whispered the word. Looking up at Ellen with angry, bloodshot eyes she said in a loud voice, accusingly, 'Why can't I have *your* baby? You don't want it and I do!'

Ellen was stunned. 'You? Have my baby?'

'And why not?' Margaret was getting hysterical. 'You're living in our house, the baby will be born in our house. Why can't you just go home and leave the baby with us? People would think it was my baby. My baby!' Her voice screeched to a crescendo.

Samuel, fearing something was amiss, rushed into the room.

'Whatever's the matter, Margaret?' he enquired. 'I could hear your voice right down the corridor.'

'I want that baby! I want that baby!' Margaret had jumped up to face her husband. It was clear to Ellen that this conversation had taken place before.

'Keep your voice down,' he hissed. 'It'll be all round the servants' quarters if you're not careful.'

'I want Ellen's baby! Why won't you let me have it?'

Samuel took his wife by the shoulder and shook her.

'Stop it, Margaret,' ordered Samuel, who was more used to dealing with troublesome railway investors than a troublesome wife. 'We've been through all this several times. We can't adopt Ellen's baby and that's that.'

'Why not? Why not? I want that baby so much!'

He shook her again. 'Be quiet woman, do you want the whole house to hear? I keep telling you,' he said through clenched teeth, 'We are not adopting a swarthy-skinned Italian baby.'

Ellen looked on in shock. So that was it! Her childless brother and sister-in-law had discussed among themselves the prospect of adopting her baby and bringing it up as their own. They were obviously desperate to get their hands on a baby. Only *this* one wasn't good enough because it was half Italian. Half foreign.

'I don't want you to have my baby,' she said angrily. 'You're not good enough for it!' Throwing down her needlework, she ran from the room.

From then on, the atmosphere was soured. Margaret could barely bring herself to speak to Ellen. And Ellen could barely bring herself to speak to her brother after what he'd said. She felt very lonely and alone.


Ellen's mother had behaved in an extraordinary manner on hearing what Archibald had worked out to save their daughter's reputation.

'So, that's the plan, Mother,' said Archibald. 'It's Ellen's decision not to marry that Italian chappie – and that's the end of the matter. She will give up the baby and no-one will be any the wiser.'

Ellen had expected her mother to curl up her lip in distaste as she usually did when anything unpleasant had to be confronted. But not this time. Her mother didn't even have that superior 'I told you so' look on her face.

'I want a little talk with Ellen,' she said quietly to her husband, adding with uncharacteristic firmness, 'Just the two of us.' Archibald took the hint and left Ellen and Elizabeth together.

'If you're going to lecture me on what a fool I've been, you can save your breath.' Ellen was not looking forward to this little *tête à tête*.

'No, dear, that's not what I was going to say.' Her mother put an arm round a startled Ellen and steered them both to the chaise longue. 'I wanted to tell you that I understand your predicament and that I feel for you. Very much.'

'Pardon?' Ellen was taken aback.

'I feel for you,' she repeated. 'You see I once had to give something up, something very dear to me and like you I went through a lot of heart-searching. I want you to know that I have never once regretted the decision I made and I know you will never regret yours.'

'What are you saying?' blurted out Ellen. 'That *you* gave up a baby?'

The familiar lip curl returned. 'No, of course not! It was something entirely different which happened many years ago. Before you were born. Before I was married. Before I met your father, even.'

Ellen was intrigued.

'So what was it? You must tell me, now that you've gone this far.'

Her mother looked furtively across the room to check the heavy oak door was firmly shut.

She lowered her voice. 'If I do tell you, you must promise never to tell anyone. Not even your father. *Especially* not your father.'

Ellen had never known her to act like this before. The woman was showing real warmth and emotion. For the first time in her adult life, Ellen actually liked her mother.

'I promise,' she whispered conspiratorially. Her mother cleared her throat.

'What I had to give up was my faith.' Her voice quavered with emotion. She reached out and clutched her daughter's hand before continuing. 'My Catholic faith.'

As she uttered the word, Ellen took a sharp intake of

breath.

'You were a *Catholic*? A *Papist*?'

Her mother nodded. 'I came from an old Lancashire Catholic family. We had kept the faith in secret for generations since the Reformation. But when my mother died only my brother remained a Catholic. My father and I gave up the faith. It was all too hard, too perilous. It was asking too much of ordinary mortals to put themselves constantly in danger of losing everything – land, position, power, even life itself – in order to remain a Catholic. For my father discovery would have meant exclusion from business and trade deals. For my part it would have meant the end to any hope of making a good marriage.'

Ellen was astounded. 'I don't know what to say, Mother.'

'That's just as it should be – you must say nothing about this matter, ever. I just wanted you to know that I too had a big decision to make. The biggest I ever made in my life. But I never regretted it. And neither will you regret your decision. Put this baby out of your mind. Never tell anyone about it, not even your future husband whoever he may be.'

Ellen had not looked that far into the future. 'I should not even tell a man I would marry that I've had a baby?'

Her mother shook her head gravely. 'Believe me, Ellen that would be the biggest mistake of your life.'

Ellen sat deep in thought.

'You said you had a brother. I always thought you were an only child,' she said reflectively. 'What happened to him, my Papist uncle?'

'He became a priest,' replied her mother. 'The foolish man.'

146

Mrs Bailey, having opened up in a way Ellen had never seen before, suddenly changed back to her old self. Standing up briskly she said to Ellen, 'That's all we'll say about this little matter. Ever.'

She walked out of the room leaving a very shaken Ellen who wasn't sure which 'little matter' her mother was referring to – Ellen's baby or her mother's Catholicism. On reflection Ellen decided she meant both.

True to her word, Mrs Bailey never again mentioned Ellen's baby, waving her off at the station the next week on her journey to London and greeting her on her return several months later. She never came to visit her daughter in London.

In fact the only family member who came to visit her was her favourite brother, Benjamin, a captain in the Coldstream Guards, whose battalion was based in London.

He always seemed so happy, so full of life. Before her pregnancy began to show he would often take her out to museums and concerts and walks in the parks. When he was with her, Ellen was able to forget her own sad predicament.

In the later stages of her pregnancy, Ben would visit her at Samuel's house whenever he could. After she'd had the baby he timed his visit with military precision. It was no coincidence that he had called in to see her on that particular day. He had learned from Samuel on which day the baby would be taken away by the childless couple.

For Ellen that day was the darkest hour of her soul. Benjamin had understood and had visited her in her hour of need.

'How terrible for you, little sister,' he said, hugging her to him. 'Jack, my best friend and a fellow officer, has just suffered the loss of a child. His little boy, a golden-haired angel from all accounts, died of the fever last month. Jack is distraught, he loved the child so much. I know you must feel the same... for you, also, it must have been like losing a baby.'

'Oh, Ben!' sobbed Ellen, 'You are the only one who knows how I feel. The only one!'

'Be a brave girl, Ellen.' Benjamin said softly, his strong arm holding her comfortingly. 'Do you remember me telling you that when you were little? When you hurt yourself falling off the rocking horse in the nursery?'

'I came off because you rocked the horse too hard for me! And I fell on your precious collection of tin soldiers and cut my leg! I remember how you picked the soldiers up before you rescued me!' Ellen threw her head back and laughed at the childhood recollection.

'That's better!' said Benjamin. 'That's the first time I've seen you laugh today.'

'It's the first time I've laughed since the fifteenth of May,' replied Ellen, referring to the day she gave birth. 'Once I'd seen my baby and knew I had to give him away without even holding him I didn't believe I'd ever smile again. Oh, Ben will I always feel this miserable? Every year on that day can you imagine how terrible it will be for me? I shall never be able to say to anyone "Today is my son's birthday".'

'I'll tell you what we'll do,' said her brother. 'Every May fifteenth you and I will go out for a celebration. No matter where I am, if at all possible I will come home on that day. We'll make it a special day. We'll go to the theatre or a concert and we'll drink a toast to him on his

148

birthday, just you and I. You are my precious little sister and I shall make sure you are never sad on that day. And that's a promise.'

With the moral support of her brother, Ellen believed that life could after all be worth living. Two hours before his arrival the childless couple, whose identity was known only to Samuel, had come by arrangement to take delivery of their new child. Ellen never saw them. She didn't even know their name. All she was told by the midwife was that they were 'nice, refined people'.

That morning her hearing was extra sensitive. It was as though she entered the room across the corridor with them as she heard their joyous cries on seeing the baby. 'Isn't he lovely,' cooed a woman's voice. 'Do let me hold him, nurse.' 'What a nice little chap you are,' said a man's voice.

'We're going to call him William, after my husband,' said the woman.

'Better give him back to nurse, Mary my dear,' said the man, 'and then let us be off. The carriage is waiting outside.'

Ellen pressed her hands against her ears in a vain effort to stop her hearing the sound of their footsteps as they took her baby away. It was a moment she would re-live time and time again, in her waking hours and in her dreams, every day of her life.

# Chapter 15

It was two years since Domenica's father and brothers had confronted Angelo and forced him to lay bare his terrible secret – that he was impotent. In the days and months that followed there had been a dramatic change in Domenica. From being a sunny, happy woman she had turned into a sad, withdrawn shadow of her former self and she had lost a considerable amount of weight.

But worse than the weight loss was the bruising. Every time her family saw her she seemed to have some new injury which she attempted to hide under her hair or shawl.

'Is Angelo beating you?' her brother Gino asked on meeting her alone in the town square.

Domenica looked at him through dead eyes and shook her head. How could she tell her brother how much her life had changed... how her husband had turned from a gentle man into a rough, violent brute?

Gino touched a large bruise on her cheek. She flinched in pain.

'What about this?' he asked.

'I keep bumping into things,' she said in a flat voice.

'I don't believe you!,' replied Gino. 'Swear on our mother's life that you did this to yourself. Swear that Angelo isn't beating you. Go on, swear it!'

Domenica dropped her head. She felt shame as well as

fear in admitting the truth to her brother.

'I thought as much,' snarled Gino. 'What a pig that man is. He may be a second cousin but he's still a pig.'

She became alarmed at the vehemence in his voice. 'You must never tell him that you know,' she said anxiously. 'He will think I told you. He will kill me if you say anything.' There was naked fear in her dark, sunken eyes. 'I am so frightened of him.'

Domenica continued to press Gino not to say anything to Angelo. She was relieved when finally he agreed to keep silent.

But things went from bad to worse as Angelo continued to abuse her – and Domenica could see the way her brother's anger rose every time he saw her trying to cover up some fresh injury.

One evening, after Gino and his brother Tonio had drunk too much wine, they made their way across the town square to Domenica's house.

It was a warm evening and the shutters had not been closed. From a vantage point outside the window they watched and waited. Angelo was seated at the kitchen table with his back to them. The remains of his supper were spread out in front of him and an empty wine goblet stood by his right hand. Domenica was clearing away the dirty dishes. As she passed him, Angelo grabbed her by the wrist.

'Get me more wine,' he ordered.

'We have none. You drank it all.' She saw the fire in his eyes and knew he would be violent with her. She tried to pull away but he tightened his grip on her wrist making her cry out with pain.

'Stop snivelling slut, whore! How dare you say I've drunk it all! Are you saying I take too much wine? You know what happened last time you said that!'

'No, Angelo don't,' Domenica whimpered as she struggled to free her wrist from his grasp. He jerked her towards him and she fell to her knees on the stone floor.

'Get me more wine!' he ordered. 'I know you've got some hidden away. Get it for me now!'

'I have none. I swear I have none.'

Domenica managed to free herself from his grasp, only to receive a hard blow to her head which sent her sprawling across the floor. She let out a scream.

'Bitch, what have I told you! Keep your voice down!'

He hit her again.

But before the beating could continue any more, there was a commotion outside and Domenica's brothers burst through the door. They grabbed hold of Angelo dragging him off his chair. With the speed of lightening Gino pulled out a knife and plunged it into his neck.

In a frenzied attack the brothers laid into him, stabbing him repeatedly till all three men, and the stone floor underneath, were covered in blood.

Domenica was cowering in the corner, her hands pressed to her face as she watched her brothers attacking Angelo. When the stabbing stopped, her husband's body lay stretched out in front of her. The stone floor, which she'd washed clean only a few hours ago, was now awash with blood. It was a scene reminiscent of an abattoir. Gino gave the lifeless form one final kick.

She screamed.

Then it was Gino's turn to say: 'Keep your voice down.'

Fleeing from the scene of the crime, Domenica and her brothers took the long way home through the back streets of the town and slipped unseen into their parents' house.

Their father was still up and greeted his bloodstained sons in horror.

'What has happened? *Madonna!* Who has done this to you? And Domenica, why are you here?'

Domenica couldn't speak. She moved her lips mutely but no words came out. She couldn't bring herself to speak about the terrible events she'd just witnessed.

'It's Angelo,' Gino said, panic creeping into his voice. 'We've killed him. What are we going to do, Papa?' Then he blurted out the whole story.

When their father had recovered from the shock he put his head in his hands to help him think. 'We have no time to lose,' he kept saying over and over again. 'No time to lose.'

After a few minutes, he seemed to have formulated a plan. First of all, he told them, they had to remove their blood-soaked trousers and shirts and wash themselves outside in water from the well. Then they must get dressed in their Sunday best, the only spare items of clothing they possessed.

Domenica had avoided getting blood on her clothes – she had been so repelled by the sight of Angelo's corpse that she couldn't bring herself to go anywhere near him. Staggering from the house, she vomited in the street before hurrying along with her brothers.

When they were clean and Domenica was calmer, all four sat down – and in a desperate frame of mind, their father told them his plan of action.

'You cannot stay in Fizzano,' he said gravely. 'You cannot stay in Italy. By tomorrow, the authorities will be searching for Angelo's killer. The first one they'll look for is you, Domenica. As his wife you might be suspected of the killing. You will all have to leave tonight.'

'Tonight!' exclaimed Gino. 'Is that possible? How will we travel?'

'I know where we can get our hands on some donkeys for the journey,' his father said. 'You will make your way to my second cousin's house in La Spezia. He owes me a favour. Then in La Spezia you must lie low until you can arrange a boat passage to England.'

'We have no money,' said Gino.

'I'll give you money,' he father said. 'Money that I've saved up for my daughters' weddings.'

Domenica couldn't bear to look at her father. She knew what a big sacrifice he was making, handing over the small amount of money he'd managed to put away for her sisters.

'In England,' her father continued, 'you will make your way to Manchester and to the house of my brother, Mario. He will shelter you and give you protection – because you're family. I would do the same for his children.'

After he'd spelt out his plan for them, her father slumped down in his chair, for all the world looking like a broken man. Domenica reached out and touched his hand.

'Papa,' she whispered.

Her father wouldn't look at her. It was as if he couldn't trust himself not to cry. 'Before you leave, say farewell to Mamma,' he said with tremulous voice.

Within weeks Domenica and her brothers had embarked on board a cargo ship carrying Carrara stone and marble destined for Liverpool. As she watched the coastline

154

disappear she felt she was putting Angelo and Italy behind her.

It had all happened so quickly – almost in the blinking of an eye. It was like a nightmare… a nightmare that would never go away. Whenever she closed her eyes she could see the blood, so much blood, covering the stone floor of her small house in Fizzano. In her dreams she tried to wash it away, mopping the floor like she did every day – or used to do. But still the blood was there… everywhere. On her hands and on her clothes as well as the floor. There didn't seem to be enough water in the whole of Italy to wash it all clean.

# Chapter 16

It was May the fifteenth, the day Ellen and Pietro's son would be two years old. True to his word, Benjamin was taking her out for their secret assignment to mark the day.

They discovered with great pleasure that the date coincided with a visit to Manchester by Charles Dickens and his troupe of amateur actors 'The Splendid Strollers' who had been performing plays throughout England for the benefit of the Guild of Literature and Art. Their tour had been enormously successful.

'Oh Ben, I'm so very happy that you were able to come home,' said Ellen giving his arm an appreciative squeeze. 'It matters so much to me that you were able to be here with me on this day of all days.'

'I wouldn't have missed it for the world,' he said, returning the squeeze. 'A promise is a promise. Any soldier knows that.'

Ellen sighed and then smiled up at him. She was truly delighted to be with her dear brother once again. His presence at the play was appreciated even more because she had not been expecting to see him in England, let alone Manchester. Two months ago, war had been declared against Russia. Ben's battalion of the Coldstream Guards had left England for their base in the Mediterranean. Ellen was convinced she was going to have to spend the anniversary on her own when, out of the blue, he turned up at Bailey's Mount.

'We were all just sitting around the barracks in Malta doing absolutely nothing so I thought I'd take a bit of home leave,' he explained to his surprised but delighted family.

'Ben,' she said as they were settling into their theatre seats, 'When do you think you'll be going to the Crimea?'

'Soon, I hope.' He spoke confidently. 'I can't wait to get at that murdering Tsar! We're all itching to get a bash at him.'

'Does that mean you might be out there next year?' Ellen asked anxiously, 'In May… May the fifteenth?'

'Good heavens, no! It'll all be over well before then. Before Christmas,' assured her brother. 'It will be a three month campaign at the most. I will be here with you on this day next year. Have no fear about that.'

The house lights went down.

'You will be careful, won't you,' Ellen said in a whisper.

'You sound like Mother,' Ben whispered back. 'She's worried I'll catch a cold in the Russian winter!'

'But I thought you said you wouldn't be there in the winter?'

'Precisely, my dear sister.' Ben patted her hand as the curtain rose.

# Chapter 17

One evening in early September, Pietro and Nello were sitting at one of the small tables outside Palomba's shop drinking a beer. They were waiting for the shop to close so that Signora Palomba and Marietta could serve them their meal. A slim woman in black with a black shawl covering her head and shoulders walked hurriedly passed them and into the shop. They caught just a brief glimpse of her face but both men recognised her immediately.

'Isn't that Domenica?' Nello asked, his eyes following her.

Pietro could not speak. His throat was dry as dust. Blood rushed from his head and boiled around his heart. He was so light-headed he knew that if he stood up he'd slither to the ground.

No such restrictions applied to Nello, however, who jumped up and followed her into the shop.

The young woman had her back to him and was speaking to Signora Palomba and pointing to a box of crystallised fruits.

'Domenica?' said Nello boldly, in a voice so loud that the woman nearly leapt out of her skin. She spun round to look at him. And then her gaze fell on the face of the man framed in the shop doorway – Pietro, who somehow had managed to overcome his temporary paralysis. Domenica blanched.

'Oh!' she blurted out, dropping the money she was proffering all over the shop counter. The three young people stared at each other as they looked from one to another.

At last Signora Palomba could stand it no longer. 'Do you want this box of fruits or shall I put it back on the shelf?' Getting no reply from the mesmerised woman and bursting with curiosity she addressed the two young men: 'Do you boys know this lady?'

'Yes,' said Nello. 'She is from our village, and ...'

'Yes, she is from our village,' Pietro jumped in, petrified Nello would spill the beans in front of his mother-in-law. 'How are you, Domenica?' he said, hoping his voice did not betray his emotions. 'How strange to meet you in Manchester.'

Strange indeed! It was four years since he'd last seen her... in Fizzano... a lifetime ago, it seemed. Was he dreaming? Could this really be the girl he'd always loved, the woman he was going to marry? He put a steadying hand on the doorframe.

Domenica dropped her eyes. 'Yes, I'm in Manchester,' she said. 'Since May.'

'Are you here on your own?' Nello asked.

'No. I'm with two of my brothers. We are staying with Uncle Mario in Spindle Street.'

'So *you* are the relatives living with the Sorettis!' exclaimed Nello. 'Your cousins told us they had family from Italy staying – but they said it was very secret, very hush-hush.'

Domenica blushed. 'I don't know why they should say that.'

'But why are you here?' asked Pietro, still in shock but nonetheless very curious.

'I am doing a message for my Aunt,' she said evasively.

'I don't mean what are you doing in this shop,' said Pietro. 'I mean what are you doing over here in England? I thought you were married. To your cousin Angelo.'

At the mention of her late husband's name, Domenica looked faint and leaned back against the counter for support. 'He is dead,' she said in a whisper.

Pietro watched her, mesmerised. After a moment's silence the Signora spoke.

'You are a widow like me,' she sighed. 'It's a very sad position to be in. How lucky that you have kind relatives to look after you.'

Domenica, leaving the money on the counter, pushed her way out of the shop and ran towards Spindle Street, leaving two very stunned young men. Nello and Pietro returned to the table where they had been drinking their beers, well out of earshot of Signora Palomba.

Nello was the first to speak.

'She is still very beautiful.'

Pietro could not trust himself to answer and turned his back on his cousin, staring down the street in the direction she had gone.

'Does Marietta know about you and your former girlfriend?' asked Nello mischievously.

'Shut up will you!'

'So you haven't told her? I guessed as much.' Nello smirked.

'I told you to shut up!' Pietro gripped his beer glass. He was very tempted to throw it at his cousin. Very tempted indeed.

'If you had told her,' Nello taunted, 'I can't imagine she'd be very thrilled to learn that the girl to whom you were engaged was now living in the next street! '

'Look, this is none of your business!' Pietro, breathing hard, moved his face close to Nello's.

'That's where you're wrong,' replied Nello. 'I am very much involved with what went on between you and Domenica. Don't ever forget that. At one time you had cause to feel extremely grateful to me for getting you out of the very big hole you'd dug for yourself. Just remember that!'

There he goes again, brooded Pietro … trying to make himself a big man. Pietro knew that deep down, Nello's baiting was motivated by jealousy. Jealousy that had eaten away at him ever since Pietro had married Marietta, the girl Nello loved. Pietro could see it in his eyes every time his cousin looked at her.

Signora Palomba interrupted their increasingly bitter conversation by running out into the street waving her hand in the air shouting 'Signora, Signora!' But Domenica was nowhere to be seen.

She turned to the boys holding out her hand with several coppers on it.

'The lady forgot this. Poor woman, she certainly didn't look as if she'd got money to throw around.'

Seizing his opportunity, Nello snatched the cash from his landlady's hand.

'I'll take it to her,' he said, hurtling off down the street towards the Sorettis' house.

When Domenica's presence in her uncle's house became known, Pietro felt obliged to confess his previous relationship to his wife. Marietta had taken it badly at first, weeping hysterically, accusing him of still yearning for his first love and refusing to listen to her husband's protestations.

'It is *you* that I am married to, it is *you* that I love,' said Pietro. 'Everything is finished between me and Domenica. I swear you have nothing to fear from her.'

'I won't have her here in this house,' sobbed Marietta. 'You and she will run off together, back to Italy!'

'Whatever gave you that idea?' Pietro asked.

'Nello told me all about the two of you! How you were childhood sweethearts. How you were going to marry her. That you and she were engaged. He told me everything!' Marietta flung herself dramatically on the bed and punched the feather pillow. 'Everything! He told me everything!'

Nello! Curse the man! Pietro might have known he was behind this outburst of Marietta's.

'It is true that we were engaged to be married but it was long before I met you.' Pietro decided not to explain the full story about Domenica. Or about Ellen ... and the baby that never was ... and all those other complications.

'Come, Marietta,' he said opening his arms to her. She went to him still weeping but not quite so hysterically as she listened to his reassurances that she was his only love.

# Chapter 18

The news from the Crimea was bad. Far from being the short three-month campaign envisaged by the generals and politicians, the slaughter and deaths from disease continued unabated throughout the autumn and winter and into another year.

Half a million men had lost their lives, among them was Captain Benjamin Bailey of the Coldstream Guards. His family learned, in the darkest month of the year, that he had been mortally injured in the useless charge of the Light Brigade and later died from his wounds.

It was a bitter winter, not only in the Crimea. At Bailey's Mount the snow lay deep. Mrs Bailey had taken to her bed on hearing the news of Benjamin's death and was still there two months later.

Ellen had reacted in a similar way to her mother, shutting herself in her room for days on end, all the time sobbing uncontrollably.

'We've all suffered, you know,' said Archibald, trying to bring his daughter to her senses. 'You've lost a dear brother, I am aware of that. What about me? You don't see me breaking down and moping all over the place, do you? I think it's high time you pulled yourself together. Life goes on.'

Ellen was made angry by his words. 'Benjamin was the only one who cared about me. The only one!'

'We all care about you, lass,' said her father. 'And we all love you.'

'You *don't* care about me or you wouldn't have done what you did!'

'What have I done?' asked a bemused Archibald. He found women very difficult to understand. There was his wife, locked away in what she called her 'boudoir', not speaking a single word to him for weeks on end, not shedding a single tear since Benjamin died. And here was his daughter blaming him for any number of unspecified wrongs. Men were so much simpler. His sons Neville, Samuel and John had reacted to their brother's death in what he would call a 'normal' way... gripping each other and their father by the shoulder and muttering phrases like 'Bad news, eh?', 'Chin up', 'Died like a hero', 'Damn proud of him, always will be'. John had announced that he had decided to study for the Anglican priesthood. He'd had it in mind for some time, he told the family, but Benjamin's death had been the final catalyst in his decision to take Holy Orders. That kind of reaction to a brother's death was quite understandable, it was sensibly sensitive, considered Archibald, without being over-sentimental.

It had been the same at the Cotton Exchange and in the Commerce Club where they all exhibited the kind of manly behaviour one could cope with. All this emotional womanly stuff was unfathomable.

'What have I done?' he repeated, putting an arm round his daughter. 'By 'eck lass you are thin,' he said feeling her bony shoulder through her dress.

She shrugged his arm away violently, 'Leave me alone! Go and talk to Mother instead. You don't mind her "moping" do you?'

'Aye, well it's different for your mother,' Archibald admitted. 'She's lost a son. It's a very different matter when you've lost a child.'

'She's not the only one. I've also lost a child!' screamed Ellen, nearly frightening the life out of Archibald with her vehemence.

'You've what?' Archibald had so successfully put the matter of Ellen's baby out of his mind that he had for the moment almost completely forgotten about it.

'A baby. I've lost a baby. My son. The son you made me give away.' She pointed an accusing finger. '*You* did. It's all your fault.'

He was open mouthed.

'If you had let me marry Pietro, given us money for a house – which you could have done – then right now I would be the mother of a child coming up for his third birthday! Your grandson, no less. And you made me give him away. I'll never forgive you for it. And now that Benjamin's gone I don't know who to turn to.'

'What on earth has Benjamin to do with it?' asked Archibald, stunned by her outburst.

'Benjamin was the only person who understood how I felt about losing my baby. The only one. The rest of the family – mother, Neville, John, Samuel, *you* – just pretended it never happened.'

'It's best that way. Best forgotten all about. Put it behind you, lass.'

'I can't do that! I will *never* forget him and I'll *never* get over Benjamin's death. He was the one person who kept me sane. Every year on May the fifteenth he promised he would come home and take me out for a celebration so at least I could tell someone "today is my son's birthday". I would have gone mad if he hadn't thrown me that lifeline.'

'I never knew,' said a solemn-faced Archibald. 'I never knew you felt like that, and I didn't know about Benjamin's promise. I'm sorry, lass. Sorry you are still so hurt after all this time.'

'All this time … It seems hardly any time at all,' she said quietly, her pent-up anger spent. She looked at him with wild eyes. 'I didn't even hold him, did you know that? Didn't even hold my own baby son.'

Her father shook his head sadly, realising for the first time that his daughter was on the verge of a nervous breakdown.

In her grief, Elizabeth Bailey too felt she was losing her sanity. For weeks on end she had not moved from her room. She had not shed a tear, nor spoken a word.

One day in early spring, while the snow was still on the ground, she noticed how the sun streaming in through the small panes of the window formed the outline of a cross on her bedroom wall. She sat up and stared at it. Silently, her lips formed the words: 'A sign from God.'

She got out of bed and knelt on the floor. The prayers of her childhood came flooding back to her. Prayers her mother had taught her.

'Gentle Jesus, meek and mild, Look on me a little child,' she mouthed involuntarily. Tears began to trickle down her cheeks. Then the floodgates opened and she was able to cry for the first time since Benjamin's death. Tears, the balm her soul needed, cascaded from her eyes. Tears that wracked her body as they healed her spirit.

For the first time in months she got dressed and went downstairs.

'I wish to go into town. Is anyone using the sociable?' she asked the surprised maid.

'No, ma'am,' she said giving a slight curtsey before rushing out to tell the driver to bring the open carriage and horse to the front door.

# Chapter 19

James Whitaker was sitting at the back of the church as usual reading his Divine Office from a battered old breviary, the book that contained the special prayers a Catholic priest is obliged to say every day.

The old priest loved to sit there after Mass with the evocative scent of incense and extinguished candles floating on the air.

He was so engrossed in his daily ritual that he did not notice an elderly lady in black entering the church. The woman was now kneeling in a bench in the first row behind the marble-topped altar railings, her head bowed low over hands clasped in prayer.

When he'd finished his priest's office he snapped the book shut and stood up. The sound startled Elizabeth Bailey who had believed she had been alone in the church. She turned to look where the noise had come from.

James was equally surprised to see such a smartly-dressed woman in his church; she looked far too well-off to be one of his own parishioners. Puzzled he walked towards her.

'I'm sorry if I interrupted your prayers,' he said, intrigued by this stranger. 'There isn't usually anyone in the church at this time of day.'

'James, is it you?' Elizabeth's voice echoed through

the church.

The priest stood stock still, towering over her. The upturned face of the woman, even through the veil of her hat, so reminded him of his late mother that he thought he was seeing an apparition. He had to clutch at the altar rail to stop himself falling over.

'I am Father James Whitaker, but who, madam, are you?'

She stood up and faced him and lifted the veil, placing it on the brim of her hat.

'James, it's me, Elizabeth,' she said. 'Your sister.'

The old priest clasped his breviary to his chest as his heart thumped so strongly he could hear the thunderous pulse in his eardrums. He felt he was dreaming, floating over the pews and rising above the marble altar.

'Oh dear,' said Elizabeth, standing up to give aid to the swaying priest. 'I didn't mean to shock you. Here, let me help you to a seat.'

'You are my sister? My little sister, Elizabeth?' His voice was faint and far away.

She nodded, holding his hand to steady him as he sat down heavily in the bench next to her.

'How did you find me ... after all these years?' he said at last, tears brimming over in his watery eyes.

'I never lost you,' she said simply.

He shook his head in uncomprehending wonder. This was the sister he had not seen for almost half a century. The sister he believed he would never see again, once he had taken the unpopular decision to become a priest.

'A priest!' exploded his father. 'Then everyone will know we are Catholics! Think how that will affect us. It will mean the end of me as a businessman. And as for your sister, it will mean the end to any hopes of her making a good marriage! So think on, James. If you want to ruin your sister's life and drive your old father to an early grave, go ahead, be a priest!'

James was heartbroken. His dear mother hardly cold and here was his father putting pressure on him to back out of the solemn death-bed promise he had given her.

'If I become a priest... no,' he corrected himself, '*when* I become a priest, I will keep away from both you and my sister,' he told his father. 'I will leave my home and my country and you will never hear from me again. I give you my word.'

It was the last time James saw his father.

'I never knew what happened to you, my little sister,' he said, his voice shaking with emotion. 'I still don't know how you found me.'

'I have always known where you were,' said Elizabeth. 'After Mother died, I knew you would go to Rome to study for the priesthood in fulfilment of the promise you gave her. Father and I never talked about you when you'd gone. But I missed you so much.'

The old priest sighed and squeezed her hand.

'When you returned to England,' continued Elizabeth, 'I followed your progress for years. Everyone in Manchester knows about you, James, and how you built this church. I even read about you in the Manchester Guardian. I was very proud.'

'But not proud enough to come and see me till now?' There was hint of criticism in his voice.

Elizabeth sighed. 'I could not come, James,' she replied, guilt welling up inside her. 'Can't you imagine how it has been for me? I married a Protestant, a very anti-Catholic Protestant. Don't be too harsh on me because I was unable to remain true to the faith.'

170

'That's where you're wrong,' said her brother. 'Don't you remember Mother saying "Once a Catholic, always a Catholic". I have prayed for you every day at Mass, you know. It seems that today my prayers have been answered.' He smiled a weary smile.

The emotion of meeting up with her long-lost brother added to the terrible burden she carried. Elizabeth could contain her grief no longer. She pulled the veil down over her face to hide the tears she could not stop.

'What is troubling you?' he asked.

'I am in torment, James. My youngest son has been killed in the Crimea,' she said. Using her handkerchief she tried to stem the flow of tears. 'Please help me with this unbearable grief. In my heart I felt God was telling me to come to you.'

He led her gently out of the church and into the adjoining priests' house. There she poured out her heart to him, reliving the lonely nights when all the grief and pain circled round her in the darkness. As they talked she began to travel the hard path back to the belief of her childhood. They prayed together.

'So many times I had prayed before but the words seemed meaningless,' she said. 'I did not believe God was listening. But finally this morning I believed He was.'

They talked quietly together, filling in the lost years, recalling old times.

'Do you remember how it used to be?' she said. 'Do you remember hearing Mass in secret in that dirty old dye-works by the River Irwell? And how Mother used to hide the priests in our house?'

'Those were the dark days, they are behind us now.'

They sat in silence for a few moments.

171

'Elizabeth,' said James, 'Do you wish to be received back into the church?'

'I cannot,' she said, struggling with her conscience. 'My husband knows nothing of this... he has no idea that he is married to a Catholic. I haven't the courage to tell him. And even though I was compelled to come here and find you, I still cannot go all the way and return to my Catholic faith completely. It troubles me, but...'

'Today you have taken that first step on the way,' he said gently, with understanding.

Bowing her head she said, 'James, will you hear my confession?'

# Chapter 20

The feelings Pietro once had for Domenica had been buried so deep in his heart he didn't know where to find them.

He was realistic enough to know that with a wife and babies to support he could not afford the luxury of living in the past, dwelling on what might have been. He'd surrounded himself with an armour of indifference and in doing so be believed that he could deaden the feelings he once had for her. But when he'd glimpsed Domenica in Palomba's shop his armour was pierced, so powerful was the impact of seeing her again. He went home that evening shaking so much Marietta thought he was starting a fever.

In the following weeks and months, Pietro went out of his way to avoid going near Spindle Street. Of course that didn't stop him from thinking about Domenica – and the fact that, instead of her being far away in Fizzano, she was now living close to him. It was something he'd longed for in previous years. But now that her closeness was a reality it was giving him nothing but pain. Pain and guilt.

He had certainly kept well away from the Sorettis' house. But – unknown to him – someone else had been beating a regular path to it. Nello.

The day his cousin went knocking on the Sorettis' door with Domenica's forgotten change was the first of many visits he was to pay her. It was the start of a secret courtship. Within a few months they were engaged to be married. Nothing gave Nello greater pleasure than the moment, at work one day, when he broke the news to Pietro.

'You're marrying Domenica?' said Pietro in disbelief.

'That's right. I'm marrying the woman you have been in love with for years. She's going to be mine! How do you feel about that?'

Pietro just didn't know how he felt about it. All he knew was he felt sick. It was as if Nello had kicked him in the stomach. The unthinkable had happened, as far as Pietro was concerned. Domenica .. *his* Domenica was marrying Nello!

'We are getting married at the end of the year,' Nello announced. 'Will you be my best man?'


Marietta stood at the scullery sink, scrubbing the grimy collars and cuffs of Pietro's and Nello's shirts. She would need to leave them soaking in the zinc bucket overnight before rinsing and hanging them out to dry first thing in the morning.

The evening meal was almost prepared apart from grating some carrots and getting the salad assembled. She was humming an Italian song to herself, one she'd heard the organ grinder playing earlier in the day in the street outside, when someone came through the front door.

'Is that you, Angelina?' she called out, thinking it

might be her sister coming in from working in the shop.

'No, it's me, Pietro,' came the reply.

Marietta grabbed the washing and dumped it in the bucket. Surely it was far too early for her husband to be coming home from work? She'd only just put the babies to bed and started on the washing!

'I haven't made the meal yet,' she said, a defensive note in her voice. She was a woman who prided herself on her housewifely skills, always keeping the house neat and tidy, the laundry beautifully done and a delicious meal ready to be placed on the table the moment her husband walked through the door. Whatever could have happened to her time-keeping today?

'Don't worry,' said Pietro, popping his head round the scullery door. 'I'm going somewhere locally, that's why I called in. I'm just going to change my work jacket.'

Pietro slipped out of the house a few minutes later, his dusty work clothes replaced by a cleaner suit. Heading towards Spindle Street he knew he was on a dangerous mission and yet he had no qualms about the risk he was taking. He was bent on confronting Domenica, determined to find out the truth. His head was still spinning from Nello's news. He'd learned from experience never to trust a word his cousin said, that his boasts were normally a bag of wind with nothing solid about them at all. But his boast about marrying Domenica had touched a raw nerve and Pietro couldn't rest until he'd had it confirmed. The only person who could do that was Domenica. In the months since he'd discovered she was now living in Ancoats, he'd given the house in Spindle Street a wide berth. He'd had enough trouble as it was convincing Marietta that he wasn't about to run away with his former fiancée and didn't want any more gossip about him and Domenica to get back to his wife.

Within minutes, Pietro was standing outside the Spindle Street house. He'd already decided what he was going to say, no matter who answered his knock.

Domenica's cousin, Philomena Sorretti opened the door.

'May I speak to Domenica, please?' Pietro asked. 'I have a message for her from Nello.'

'Yes, come in,' Philomena said.

He followed her inside and found himself facing Domenica. She was seated at the kitchen table, chopping up vegetables.

She seemed startled to see him. 'Oh,' she uttered involuntarily.

Pietro scraped his throat nervously. 'I have a message from Nello,' he said, avoiding making eye contact with her.

'Yes? What is it?' She carried on chopping the vegetables. Pietro noticed that her hands were shaking.

'It's nothing serious,' he said, casting a look in Philomena's direction. He was hoping to be left alone with Domenica, but that was obviously not going to happen. He could tell from the way Philomena had settled herself down in the rocking chair and was gazing at the two of them.

'It's nothing serious,' Pietro repeated, 'but it is a bit personal. Is there somewhere we can talk? The parlour?' he ventured.

'We don't have a parlour!' Philomena snorted. 'That's the room my mother uses when she takes in washing. It's always piled high with sheets, and dirty laundry soaking in the bath tub. If you go in she'll make you give her a hand with the mangle!' Domenica scooped up the chopped vegetables and dropped them into the cooking pot. She shot Pietro a glance.

'I'm going to church shortly,' she said. 'You can walk along with me and tell me Nello's message.'

She slipped her shawl over her head and shoulders and left the Sorettis' house, followed by Pietro.

'I often call in at church at this hour of the day,' she said, talking to him as if they'd chatted like this every day of the week. 'It's not so crowded as it is during Mass. I like to sit quietly on my own, saying my prays and thinking about… well, everything really.'

They walked briskly along the street towards St Agnes's. Pietro remained silent.

'What was the message from Nello?' she asked.

'There is no message.'

Pietro kept on walking. Domenica tried to match his stride but ended up having to run to catch him up.

'No message! Then what is this all about?'

By now, they had reached the church door. He turned to face her. 'I think you know what all this is about, Domenica. I want a talk with you. It's about time we had a talk, don't you think?'

'If you say so,' she replied, her eyes holding his. She looked proud, haughty almost, as she arranged her shawl making sure her hair was completely covered before entering the church.

Their eyes took a moment to adjust to the gloom inside.

'Why are you marrying Nello?' demanded Pietro under his breath. 'You can't possibly marry him. You must realise that!'

Domenica stiffened. 'It's none of your business. None

of your business at all.' She turned red eyes on him. 'You had your chance to marry me and you let it go. You let me go! You have absolutely no right to tell me what I can or cannot do!'

'But you don't love him!' protested Pietro. 'You'll be marrying him for the wrong reason. You're marrying him just to teach me a lesson! That's why you're doing it. To hurt me and to spite me.'

Domenica sighed, exasperated. 'Why do men think the world revolves around them and them alone? I may be marrying Nello for the wrong reason but it's got nothing to do with hurting you. I am not trying to teach you a lesson or to spite you.'

'Then why are you doing it? It doesn't make sense to me. You've virtually admitted that you don't love him.'

'Ah, love! What is that, I wonder?' she said in a small voice.

'It's what we had, Domenica. In Italy…when first I saw you in the village square. That was love.'

'So why didn't you marry me?' Her words were sorrowful, pathetic, all her haughtiness gone as she fought back tears. 'Why didn't you come back for me? I waited for you. I waited for you for so long!'

Pietro put his arm round her and pulled her to him gently.

'I am to blame,' he said. 'I made a terrible mistake. I didn't know what I was doing, I promise you. It just happened. And then I thought this person was having my baby and of course I had to do the honourable thing and agree to marry her.'

'I know all this,' whispered Domenica against his shoulder.

'It turned out she wasn't having a baby after all.'

Pietro's words were bitter. 'But she might just as well have because by then you'd got married. I thought my heart would break.'

'But you love Marietta and the *bambini*,' ventured Domenica. 'You must be happy now.'

Pietro said nothing for a few moments. Then he spoke.

'Being happy isn't the same as being in love.'

'Yet you wouldn't leave Marietta and the children and run away with me, would you?' she breathed in his ear.

There was a long silence. The only sound was the creaking of the heavy oak door as the lone worshipper went out of the church.

'Are you asking me to do that?'

'What if I did?' she murmured.

'It isn't fair to ask such a thing,' Pietro said. 'They are my family.'

'And I am not.' She sighed deeply. 'If it's any consolation, Pietro, I do not love Nello. But he's a good man, I think. I will be able to leave my Uncle's house and that is my main reason for wanting to marry Nello. I can't bear living under their roof for a moment longer than I have to. And I cannot go back home to Italy. So you see, I have very little choice.'

She sat up and adjusted her shawl once again. 'It will be a quiet wedding. Just the two of us and our witnesses.'

'I won't be coming,' Pietro said decisively. 'I told Nello quite definitely. I shall stay well away.'

'I understand,' she said, rising to leave.

Pietro remained in the bench and knelt down in the pew. He felt an icy cold blanket settle on his mind, freezing it. He said his prayers for several minutes after she'd gone. Then he got up, brushed the dust from his knees and walked slowly back towards his own home and Marietta.

# Chapter 21

Domenica and Nello were married quietly and without fuss – as befitted the remarriage of a widow. The marriage service was conducted by the elderly Father Whitaker.

The newly-weds rented a house in Ancoats in one of the streets near the Rochdale canal – far enough away from Domenica's troublesome relatives in Spindle Street.

'I hated it in that house,' she told Nello. 'Uncle Mario is a brutal man. I find him very frightening.'

'Did he hit you?' Nello asked his new wife. 'I will go and punch him in the face if he did.'

'He didn't hit me,' Domenica replied. 'But I saw him threatening other people. It was a horrible house to live in. Especially after my brothers left to go to America. I felt very alone.'

Nello puffed himself up, beating his fist on his chest. 'You need have no fear any more – now that you are married to me. I will protect you. I am strong and brave.'

Domenica, who by now had become accustomed to Nello's boastful nature, was nonetheless grateful for her new husband's outburst. She missed her father and brothers... in fact she missed her whole family. And Italy. She missed the sunshine and warmth and the clean, sweet air.

Nello was delighted to be married to Domenica – for a number of reasons. One of the most pleasurable ones was knowing that he had won Pietro's woman – especially as his cousin had stolen Marietta, the woman Nello loved. He was also delighted by the unexpected discovery – on their wedding night – that Domenica was still a virgin.

'But you've been married before!' he said expressing great surprise.

Domenica remained silent, turning over on her side now that she knew what her father had meant when he talked about Angelo making a woman of her. It was Nello, not Angelo who did it.

'Wasn't your first husband able to do what I've just done?' Nello asked.

'No,' muttered Domenica into her pillow, revisited by the shame she had felt years ago.

'And presumably Pietro didn't do it to you, either?'

The smugness in Nello's voice was too much for Domenica. She turned over in bed to face him.

'No! And don't you ever suggest such a thing again about me and Pietro!'

Nello smiled to himself in the dark. 'You have made me very happy, Domenica, to know that I have not married second-hand goods. You could make me even happier by telling me that you never loved Pietro.'

Domenica turned her back on him again and buried her face in the pillow. Hot tears soaked into the linen pillowslip. How she wished she could have said those words that Nello was longing to hear. How she wished.

Within a few months of their marriage, Domenica realised that she had married a man who drank to excess.

Nello's binges were every bit as frequent as Angelo's but there was a big difference. Whereas Angelo became violent through drink, Nello just became drunk. Almost every evening after his day's work he would settle down to consuming vast quantities of alcohol.

It was a disappointment to Domenica. She imagined that the two of them would spend cosy evenings by the fire, telling each other about the day's events, exchanging bits of gossip. Instead – after he'd eaten the meal that she always had ready and waiting for him when he walked in the door – he would settle down with a couple of bottles of red wine and proceed to drink most of it. His conversation consisted mainly of telling her how magnificent he'd been at his job that day and how much better than all the other stoneworkers he was. Quite soon the alcohol would get to his tongue and he'd begin to slur, his words becoming incomprehensible. The evening would draw to a close with Nello lying slumped in his chair, snoring loudly.

# Chapter 22

The sight of her mother's frail figure drooping in the bath chair made Ellen want to weep. She knew the time was very close when her mother would be confined to her bed and that death was not far away. In the year since the diagnosis of her incurable tumour, Elizabeth Bailey's health had deteriorated rapidly.

Ellen tucked the blanket round the thin body before pushing her seventy-year-old mother on her daily outing.

'Come, Mother,' said Ellen brightly as she pushed her round the leafy paths in the garden at Bailey's Mount. 'The fresh air will do you good. Just once more round the rose garden.'

Archibald Bailey, although a year older than his sick wife, was himself in the rudest of health and only in the last few weeks had he accepted that his wife was dying. It was a reality he nevertheless managed to push to the back of his mind … something he would deal with when the time came. The distressing spectacle of his wife fading away before his eyes was matched, however, by an improvement in his daughter's health.

In the years following Benjamin's death, Ellen had suffered from a variety of illnesses which her father suspected were of nervous origin. Her joints ached and painful red blotches appeared on her skin. She would come downstairs and lie on the sofa all day, too fatigued to do anything.

At first Archibald imagined he could make her 'snap out of it', but as time wore on, far from getting better Ellen added a nervous tic to her other ailments. His bright-eyed little daughter had turned into a morose, neurotic woman.

Two years ago she became so unwell Archibald thought she might benefit from the 'cold-water treatment'. Under her brother John's protection she was sent to a fashionable hydropathic establishment in Yorkshire. After that visit there was a slight improvement in her mental state, but when the dreaded anniversary of May the fifteenth came round all the good work came unravelled.

'What a waste of brass,' complained Archibald to Neville. His eldest son had been put in full charge of Bailey's mills in anticipation of Archibald's retirement. He still planned to keep an eye on the business from home, just calling into the mills 'from time to time, say three times a week' he told Neville, ominously. It was going to be many years, feared Neville, before he would have a completely free hand with the business without his father peering over his shoulder.

'It's worth spending any amount of money if it means getting Ellen better,' said Neville in an uncharacteristic outpouring of generosity of spirit.

'Aye,' said Archibald, 'if those charlatans *can* make her better. I've shelled out money left, right and centre – and now there's some daft quack in Harley Street I'm supposed to fork out for.'

Neville was anxious that his father should spend money more freely. In doing so it might encourage the old man to take a more relaxed attitude towards Neville if

185

he ever discovered the large amounts of 'hidden expenses' his son was helping himself to on a regular basis to enhance his increasingly grand lifestyle and for the upkeep of his imposing new Cheshire mansion.

When the time came, it wasn't Archibald's daughter who was taken to Harley Street for a consultation but his wife. The diagnosis was bad; she had less than a year to live.

Her mother's strength and courage in dealing with her illness had a remarkably restorative effect on Ellen.

'It's an ill wind,' observed the maid to the cook. 'Miss Ellen is almost back to her old self now that the Mistress is so poorly.'

As Ellen gently moved her mother from the bath chair onto the sofa she realised this would probably be the last time she would be taking her outside for her morning constitutional. Getting her up and dressed, moving her from chair to sofa and back to bed was exhausting the sick woman and was doing her more harm than good.

Ellen took the icy cold hand between her own. 'Would you like to go to bed, Mother?'

'Yes … please,' she said, her breathing heavy and laboured.

Two months later, the doctor advised Archibald that his wife had only hours to live. The whole family were summoned to the bedside to say goodbye.

John, who had taken Holy Orders the previous year, travelled from his parish in Macclesfield. Neville and Lucy brought their two children. Samuel and Margaret came up on the train from London.

As their mother's life was drawing to a close, she began to talk in a stronger voice than previously.

'I would like a priest,' she said to the hushed family group.

'Your son John is here, Mother,' said Archibald. 'Sit next to her, John. She obviously wants to talk religious stuff for a while.'

But Elizabeth waved her bony hands saying, 'Not John … I want a *real* priest.'

'Well, I'll be blowed,' gasped Archibald. 'After all the money I spent getting the lad to ordination and his mother says he's not a real priest! I suppose she still thinks of him as a little boy. We'd best send for the minister if that's what she wants.'

In the deep recesses of her mind, Ellen dredged up a conversation of nine years ago. A conversation she had not thought about since with so many other emotional and traumatic events having taken place in the intervening years.

Her mother continued to wave her hands about in an agitated way. 'I want a priest,' she said, 'A *real* priest! Not a minister!'

'Whatever is she talking about?' questioned Samuel, wondering if his mother was hallucinating in her final hours.

'I think your mother's rambling a little,' replied Margaret in a low voice, touching her head with an index finger. 'She doesn't know what she's talking about, that much is clear.'

Hearing her sister-in-law dismissing her mother as a simpleton, Ellen jumped to her defence.

'She's not rambling! She knows exactly what she's talking about. And so do I.'

All eyes were on Ellen.

'Tell them what kind of priest you want, Mother,' she

said gently, stroking the paper-thin skin on the back of the old lady's hands.

'I want a Catholic priest,' she said firmly.

The room fell silent, but not for long.

'A what?' boomed Archibald, Neville and Samuel in unison.

'Mother is a Papist,' said Ellen, pleased at the effect this information produced. 'That is why she wants a Catholic priest … I will take the sociable and go and fetch one.'

'*You* know where to find a Popish priest?' Archibald was incredulous. He didn't know which was the most staggering piece of news – that his wife to whom he'd been married for forty-five years was, unknown to him, a Papist … or that his neurotic daughter knew where to find a Popish priest!

Ellen left the bedroom and within minutes was on her way to Ancoats, to the parish church of St Agnes. This was the only Catholic church Ellen had any knowledge of, from the one visit she paid it with Pietro when they were discussing marriage with the nice old priest. She couldn't remember his name – and he was probably dead by now. Even so, she was sure she'd be able to find a Catholic priest to visit her mother from the church in Ancoats.

But James Whitaker wasn't dead – elderly and frail but very much alive as he climbed into the Bailey's open carriage.

'Would the family leave the room for a short while,' said Father Whitaker, putting on his priestly attire in preparation for giving the Last Rights to Elizabeth Bailey – the sacrament of Extreme Unction.

Waiting on the landing outside the bedroom, the family – all except Ellen – were in a state of shock.

'Well I'll be damned!' said Neville. 'My own mother a Papist!'

Archibald, who had calmed down, approached Ellen in a more thoughtful frame of mind.

'You knew didn't you, lass?'

'Yes, Father.'

'How long? How long has she been a Papist and how long have you known?'

Ellen didn't answer immediately. She dropped her eyes to her clasped hands in an uncharacteristic moment of reticence. The pleasure she'd initially taken in announcing her mother's true religion was eking away. Her father was about to receive a really big shock and she was beginning to feel sorry for him.

'She told me some years ago that she'd been born into a Catholic family,' said Ellen in a low voice. 'Mother said that life was all about making choices… and that just as I had chosen to give up my baby she had chosen to give up her religion.'

At the mention of the baby, Margaret shot her a poisonous look.

'At least Mother can get her religion back again,' said Ellen, her voice tinged with bitterness, 'which is more than can be said for my son. He is lost and gone forever.'

Archibald's eyes clouded.

'Lass, you're not still going on about that, are you? It's been eating away at you all these years and I'm blowed if I know what to do about it. And I'm blowed if I know what to do about all this mumbo jumbo going on in there,' he said, indicating the room where a priest was blessing and anointing his own sister, hearing her confession and giving her Holy Communion.

'I really think, Father,' said Ellen, 'there is nothing you can do about Mother. Let's be thankful that she will be dying a happier woman than if you'd denied her last request.'

'That's all very well,' said Archibald, 'but what's going to happen when word of this gets out … that a Popish priest has been seen entering and leaving Bailey's Mount? How d'you think that'll go down in the Commerce Club?'

'God moves in mysterious ways,' said John ignoring his father's self-centred reaction.

# Chapter 23

'Please hurry, Father! I do so hate being late for concerts.' Ellen was standing on the doorstep tapping her foot impatiently.

Since the death of her mother, Ellen and her father spent a good deal of time in each other's company, visiting exhibitions, attending plays and concerts. It was in these ways that the two remaining occupants of Bailey's Mount passed the days now that time hung heavily on their hands – on Archibald's hands in particular.

Five years had gone since he had finally been persuaded by Neville that his presence was no longer required on a regular basis at the mills. Now, aged eighty, he was still mentally alert and in reasonable health – but far too slow for Ellen's liking.

'Stop fretting,' said her father, shuffling along at his chosen pace. 'The carriage won't start without us.'

'No, but Mr Hallé will,' replied Ellen, handing him his hat and gloves. 'And you know tonight is my special night. You haven't forgotten?'

'How could I forget. You've reminded me of it often enough. May the fifteenth is a date that is imprinted on my memory for all time, you have made sure of that.'

'And you know what we have to say, don't you?'

The old man heaved himself into the carriage with the

help of the driver, landing heavily on the padded leather seat.

He sighed and patted his daughter's hand. 'Yes, lass. I'll not forget.'

It was a ritual father and daughter had gone through in the years following Benjamin's death. Archibald had taken his son's place as the person with whom Ellen could celebrate her son's birthday – and with whom she would drink a glass of wine sometime during that day, saying 'Today my son would be ...' naming the age her lost baby would have now reached. Today he would have been eighteen.

Archibald had gone along with this farce in order to save his daughter's sanity which he thought was borderline at the best of times.

As they settled themselves in the best seats in the dress circle, Archibald handed Ellen the programme. 'Here, lass, your eyesight is better than mine. You read what delights Mr Hallé has in store for us tonight. Did I hear someone say summat about Mr Handel's Messiah?'

'You know perfectly well that was last month,' said Ellen speaking to her father as if he were an imbecile. 'Tonight it's your favourite Beethoven oratorio, Mount of Olives.' She fumbled in her pocket. 'I remembered to bring the opera glasses. I love to see the soloists up close.'

'Well don't bother passing them to me, I'm just going to shut my eyes and let it waft over me.'

He'll fall asleep as usual, predicted Ellen. No wonder he couldn't remember which concerts he'd been to in recent months. Still, it was a comfort having her old father to go with, particularly tonight, always a difficult time – when joy and despair visited her in equal measure.

Joy, as she recalled that one precious moment when she looked into her baby's eyes... then all the years of despair that followed.

True to form, as the concert got underway, her father began to nod off. Lifting the opera glasses to her eyes she studied the faces of the orchestra and the singers. The soloists were standing a little apart from the main chorus. The young man singing the tenor solo caught her attention. He was tall and dark and had a most beautiful voice.

The concert continued and Ellen settled down to enjoying the uplifting music and the soaring voices of the singers. She closed her eyes for a moment, the blissful sounds transporting her far away from the centre of Manchester. At a pause in the oratorio she opened her eyes and looked softly on the sleeping face of her father. She smiled indulgently.

Sighing contentedly, she picked up the opera glasses once again. She scanned the orchestra and the distinguished figure of the conductor. Then she looked closely at the chorus and the soloists, pausing for a few moments on the face of the young tenor. She moved the focusing wheel to make his face sharper. Then her heart missed a beat and she gripped the glasses in a white-knuckle grasp.

Ellen was transported back in time ... it was *his* face. The young tenor soloist was the image of Pietro Falgoni.

'Father,' she whispered hoarsely, jolting the old man's arm. 'Father, wake up.'

He awoke with a loud grunt that made the woman in front turn round and glare at them.

'Look', hissed Ellen, handing him the glasses. 'Look at the young man standing to the right of the chorus master.' She forced him to take the glasses and look through them. 'Who does he remind you of?'

'Nobody. Nobody at all. He's just a young man,' he said grumpily.

'He's just like *him*,' she hissed. 'Just like Pietro.'

Their stage whispers were now becoming so loud several other people turned round and said 'Shhh..'

Archibald, annoyed at being woken up, annoyed at being shushed, handed the glasses back to his daughter ungraciously.

'You're causing a palaver. Give over, Ellen.'

'But it *is* like him, Father. It *is*.' she said, regardless of the tutting in the row in front.

'If you say so, lass, then I suppose it is.' Anything to shut her up, thought Archibald. 'But who the devil this "Pietro" is I've not the faintest idea!'

Ellen sighed exasperatedly. 'Pietro Falgoni,' she hissed in his ear. 'The stonemason.' When her father didn't immediately respond, she hissed even closer to his ear: 'The father of my baby!'

'Oh him!' replied Archibald.

'After the concert, will you come with me to the stage door and find out.'

'What are you on about?' Archibald was finding this exchange very tiresome especially as some people *two* rows ahead were now turning round and shushing them.

'I want to know if that young man is my son!' Ellen's eyes had a wild look about them. He recognised that look... she always had it just before one of her breakdowns... and he realised he'd have to calm her down by giving in to whatever it was she wanted – and sort everything out later.

He patted her hand. 'Yes, lass. But just enjoy the

concert for now.'

Ellen did not know how she managed to contain herself for the rest of the evening's performance. She was in such a state of high excitement her nervous tic returned.

As they left the crowded concert hall, Archibald decided he must have a stern word with his daughter as she seemed to be going off at the deep end once again. Indeed she seemed to be hallucinating about her lost son. He decided to try and reason with her.

'It's most unlikely that he will be your son, you know that don't you?' he said, moving at his usual slow pace.

'Stranger things have happened!' replied Ellen, raising her voice above the chattering of the crowd.

'Do you really think it's a good idea to go to the stage door? Let's get on home and discuss it there. Be a good lass, Ellen.'

But it was no good. She was convinced she had found her long-lost child.

'This is madness,' said Archibald as Ellen, linking her arm in his, marched him into the street and towards the performers' exit. 'You'll just stare at the young man and make a fool of yourself. For goodness sake, whatever you do, don't throw yourself on the lad saying that you're his mother! Imagine what a melodramatic scene that would make! This fantasy of yours is all very well but what on earth do you know about him after all this time? Absolutely nothing!'

'I know that his name is William,' she said stubbornly. 'And I know the names of his adoptive parents because I heard them talking in the corridor as they took him away.'

'And what are they?'

'William and Mary,' she said triumphantly.

'Good heavens!' exclaimed Archibald. 'I should think half the population in England have parents called William and Mary!'

Archibald and Ellen made their way through the stage door and, with the help of a generous tip, secured the services of a doorman. He led them to a room where the some of the choir and the soloists were gathered enjoying a relaxing glass of wine after the concert.

A young man was summoned over and introduced to Archibald and Ellen.

'I hope you enjoyed the concert,' he said politely, having been told, erroneously, that Archibald was one of the concert benefactors. 'Would you care to join us in a glass of Madeira? We're having a small celebration.'

'That's very kind,' said Archibald, never one to refuse a glass of Madeira wine. 'Will your daughter join us as well?' he asked Ellen.

'Yes thank you… William,' she replied.

The young man was pleased that this well-heeled lady called him by his name. She had obviously had made a point of finding out the names of that evening's soloists. 'How flattering that you know my name, ma'am – fame at last!' he jested. 'But please call me Billy. Everyone does. I'll just get your wine. I'm very glad you both can join me because I'm celebrating my first solo appearance as a concert tenor.'

'It's also your eighteenth birthday, isn't it?' said Ellen.

Once again he stopped in his tracks and stared at her in complete astonishment.

'Ah, you've been talking to my father, haven't you?' said Billy, voicing the most obvious explanation for these two strangers knowing about him. 'I'll call him across to join us as you seem to know him.'

Billy gesticulated to a distinguished-looking grey-haired man in the far corner of the room.

'Don't say anything, Ellen. Leave the talking to me,' warned her father under his breath as they could see the man pushing his way through the crowded room towards his son.

'Here are some friends of yours, Father,' said Billy, indicating the Baileys standing by his side.

'I've got a terrible memory,' said Billy's father politely, 'I seem to have forgotten your names.'

'Bailey,' said Archibald holding out his hand. 'And this is my daughter, Ellen.'

'And you don't know us,' said Ellen. 'Your son was jumping to the wrong conclusion.'

Archibald gave Ellen a warning look knowing she was about to step into dangerous territory. But he could tell from the fire in her eyes there would be no stopping her. He felt almost sorry for the young man and his father smiling so politely at them. Any minute now their cosy little world was going to be torn apart.

'You see, there's something I need to tell you,' said Ellen. Archibald closed his eyes. It was like watching a wolf pounce on a couple of lambs.

'I am Billy's mother.'

Billy was the first to recover from the shock of this statement and believing it was meant as a joke, replied, 'That is not a decent thing to say, ma'am. In case you have not heard, my own dear mother passed away last year.'

Billy was about to turn on his heels and leave this strange, mad woman well alone, when his father put a restraining hand on him.

'My name is William Ashworth,' said the older man. 'Whom, may I ask, are you?'

'I am Ellen Bailey. I gave birth to the boy you now call your son and to my eternal regret I gave him away. I gave him away to you, Mr Ashworth, eighteen years ago.'

'Father, the woman is clearly mad,' said Billy between clenched teeth. 'Let's move away quickly.'

Mr Ashworth didn't move a muscle. He didn't speak. He stood stock-still like a statue.

'I'm speaking the truth aren't I, Mr Ashworth?' persisted Ellen. 'You and your wife Mary collected my baby from a house in London in May, 1852.'

'Tell her she's speaking rot, Father,' Billy interjected. 'You and mother didn't adopt me! The woman's clearly mad.'

Ashworth cleared his throat. 'I am not prepared to discuss such personal matters in public. Is there somewhere more private we can go?'

Archibald, who had remained silent throughout this exchange, announced, 'Come back to Bailey's Mount with us. I've a carriage waiting outside. All this standing about is bringing on my gout.'

'I didn't know you had gout, Father,' said Ellen with concern.

'Well I have now,' he said crossly. 'And it's all your fault.'

Travelling in the open carriage with the Baileys to their house in Northenden, Billy and his father sat next to each other staring grimly ahead. When they arrived at Bailey's Mount they were conducted into the library.

Billy, in a confused and nervous state, still managed to take in all the details of his surroundings. The library, he noted, was a very garish room, decorated in a style he considered vulgar. Everything was new and expensive. Not a stick of antique furniture was in evidence, nor a hint of the subtle colours of the faded silk drapes and rugs from the Ashworths' fifteenth century family home in Macclesfield. In fact, from what he'd seen so far of Bailey's Mount, he thought it was the embodiment of a *nouveau riche* mansion – flashy and tasteless. He had been to homes like this before when visiting school-friends whose fathers had made their wealth from the new industries of cotton manufacture and railways. He did not despise those boys and their families, he just felt sorry for them. But right now, sitting in the tasteless opulence of the Bailey's library, he was feeling more than a little sorry for himself.

His father was tense and pale, nervously clutching at the arms of a green leather chair. Opposite them the elderly Mr Bailey was stroking his daughter on the hand as if to calm her down, like one did to a nervous horse. Miss Bailey, a plump woman of around forty years, Billy guessed, was perched on the edge of her chair staring at him in a most off-putting way. She was like a greyhound waiting to be let out of a trap.

Archibald cleared his throat. 'Hang on a minute, Ellen. Don't say owt yet,' he warned.

Billy jumped up.

'Will someone please tell me what is going on? My father and I will leave if no explanation is immediately forthcoming.'

No-one spoke, so Billy continued, his confusion rapidly turning to anger. 'Who will tell me what is happening?'

'I will,' said Ellen.

Everyone turned to face her. She didn't speak for a moment or two. The ticking of the pendulum clock was the only sound to be heard.

'Many years ago,' she began, her eyes cast downward, 'I was in love with someone I could not marry. I had a child… a boy.. and I gave him away.'

She took a deep breath and looked directly at Billy. 'I believe you are that child. My brother in London arranged for a childless couple to take you and bring you up as their own. It was the most terrible thing I ever did, to give you away. I have regretted it every moment since. Now, each year on the anniversary of your birth I celebrate that special day. Tonight at the concert I was looking through my opera glasses and knew it was you!' Her voice had risen to a crescendo.

'You're barmy, Ellen,' her father interrupted, exasperated. 'Quite barmy. What on earth must these two respectable men think of your hysterical outburst?'

'Quite so, madam!' Billy exploded. 'This is preposterous! How can you possibly think I am your child?'

'Because you are the image of your father. Your *real* father!' Ellen replied dramatically.

Billy turned to his father. 'Is this true?'

William Ashworth did not trust himself to speak, but just nodded.

'My God in heaven!' Billy exclaimed, the colour draining from his face. 'How can this be true? This is a nightmare and I shall wake up from it any minute!'

'Billy, it is true,' said William, speaking quietly and with dignity.

The young man put his hands up to his face.

'Your mother and I longed for a child,' his father told him. 'After many years we heard through a business contact that a baby from a good family was shortly to be born. We travelled down from Macclesfield and collected you along with your wet nurse.' As he spoke the colour began to return to his cheeks. His accent was cultured and smacked of breeding.

'You are from Macclesfield?' asked Archibald in surprise. 'What line of business are you in?' he enquired bluntly.

'I am a silk merchant,' replied Ashworth. 'My son …' He hesitated over the word, '…my son is following me into the family business. But he is also blessed with beautiful singing voice. He is very musical and his mother and I gave him every opportunity to develop his talent. We shall just have to wait and see which career wins out in the end, silk or singing.'

As he spoke a strange calmness came over Ellen. Billy was her son but he was also very much the son of his adopted father. She felt a sea of gratitude wash over her, gratitude that her baby had found such a loving family in which to grow up. The guilt she felt in letting him go was beginning to melt away. In its place came a different emotion… a feeling of great sympathy for the man who had believed he would always be known as Billy's father. What torment he must be going through imagining that his son might wish to desert him and find his real father! Her sympathies were confirmed when she saw his reaction to Billy's next question.

'If you are my mother,' said Billy in a tortured voice, 'then who is my father?'

As he spoke the words, Ellen shot a glance at

Ashworth. The man had closed his eyes as if in prayer. When he opened them Ellen could see the pain and suffering inside. She was filled with compassion for him.

'He is dead,' she lied. 'He died many years ago, soon after you were born.'

Ashworth gave a sigh of relief. He looked at Ellen with appreciation. Thank you, his eyes told her. Thank you, even if you are lying.

# Chapter 24

Scarcely ten miles from the centre of Manchester is the upland of the Central Pennines that rise abruptly to heights exceeding two thousand feet. And nestling in the Pennines, the mountain range that forms the backbone of England, is the ancient town of Macclesfield on the banks of the River Bollin.

Macclesfield had been a silk town for over two hundred years and the family of William Ashworth had been connected with the silk trade for virtually all of that time.

Generations of Ashworths had worked in silk.

William Ashworth had amassed a considerable fortune but was not ostentatious in the spending of it. He lived in the modestly but tastefully furnished 15th century Wunderley Hall, set on a hillside surrounded by farmland and overlooking Macclesfield forest.

All things considered, he was a happy and contented man.

There had been sadness in his life. His first wife, Mary, was unable to have children and this was a great cause of unhappiness to both of them. But then the baby boy they'd been able to adopt they had brought up as their own son. They had told no-one about the adoption and in time they themselves had come to believe that young Billy was their own flesh and blood – although one or two people in the town did remark on the child's dark eyes and raven hair and the fact he looked so unlike William and Mary who each had blue eyes and fair complexions.

When the boy had barely reached manhood, his beloved Mary died. William threw himself with even greater vigour into his work, accepting an invitation from the Secretary of State for India to visit Kashmir and report on the area's silk growing potential.

He'd been in the middle of writing his report on the trip – 'Jottings on the Mulberry Tree and the Kashmir Climate' – when he allowed himself a moment of relaxation to go and see his son sing the tenor solo on his eighteenth birthday at the Free Trade Hall in Manchester. It would be the first concert he had attended since his wife's death the previous year.

He had hoped that Billy would soon grow out of this 'singing passion' and would enter the silk trade like generations of Ashworths had done. He longed to take Billy round to all his workers and customers and introduce him as 'the next Mr Ashworth'.

'You can choose any branch of the silk business you like,' he had said, hoping to persuade the young man to go into trade instead of the arts.

'But I want to be a singer,' replied Billy stubbornly.

'There have been Ashworths in silk in Macclesfield for two hundred years. Can't you see it's your destiny?' he asked more in sorrow than in anger.

Billy had been having these conversations regularly with his father since he was fifteen and had first broached the subject of a career in music. When his mother died his father seemed to drop the subject for a while, not wishing to bring a sour note into the father-son relationship. And when he agreed to come and see him on stage that night at the Free Trade Hall in his first major solo role, Billy was almost believing that his father had accepted the idea that he would not be following him into silk.

It was certainly a night to remember, but not for the singing. Looking back he could hardly remember a single moment of the two hours on stage. That experience had been totally eclipsed by the few moments when a complete stranger had announced that she was his real mother!

A few weeks after this traumatic event, Billy suddenly decided to give up his ambition to become a famous singer and announced his intention to enter the silk trade. Perversely, found he found that he truly wanted to become part of his adoptive father's family. It was as if, somehow, he needed to prove that he was a 'true Ashworth'. After all, he'd had it drummed into him since childhood that 'Ashworths are in silk, always have been'.

His father was, needless to say, completely delighted. Fortune appeared to be shining on their family once again after the loss of the much-mourned Mary.

The night of the Free Trade Hall concert marked a turning point in other ways, too, for soon afterwards William Ashworth began to court Ellen Bailey. It was not to be a rushed affair. They were both mature people and a long courtship suited them very well. However, after four years, they eventually decided to get married, and Ellen Bailey became the second Mrs William Ashworth.

# Chapter 25

On Pietro and Marietta's twenty-fourth wedding anniversary, Signora Palomba was taken ill and died within hours. It was a great shock to everyone, and in particular to Marietta who missed her mother terribly. For weeks afterwards, Marietta would burst into tears for the slightest reason, and often for no reason at all.

'You need to get out of the house more,' Pietro told her. 'Go into town and buy yourself something nice.'

'I'll be all right soon enough,' replied Marietta as she stared aimlessly out of the window.

Pietro was in a hurry to leave for work, but he stayed on a few minutes longer. He was becoming concerned about the change that had come over his wife in recent months. The last of their six children had left home and, even though at least one of them called in to see her every day, Marietta was very aware that she had an empty nest. She'd started to act in very strange ways, fretting over incidents and worries from the past... things that were best left alone.

There had been a terrible scene last night between the two of them. Out of the blue, she accused Pietro of 'carrying on' with Domenica.

'That's ridiculous!' answered Pietro. 'Of course I haven't been carrying on with my cousin's wife!'

'But you did love her once!' accused Marietta. 'You

were engaged to be married to her!'

'There's no point in raking over the embers of the past,' said Pietro, holding his temper in check. The mention of Domenica had roused feelings in him that he preferred to leave buried. He was furious that his wife should bring it all up again – particularly when she had no grounds for doing so.

'How can I truly believe you? I know what Italian men are like!' She was working up to full-blown hysteria. 'You don't deny that you loved her, do you? No! So how do I know you and she aren't lovers now? She only lives in the next street, after all. How do I know you haven't been lovers for years!'

'What do I have to do to convince you that it's not true?' he answered patiently. He was beginning to get used to his wife's outbursts. Was it her age, perhaps? He'd heard that women 'went a bit funny' around her time of life. At a similar age, the wife of a barman from The Red Dragon had gone completely off her head and thrown herself into the Rochdale Canal. He didn't want Marietta doing anything like that.

'Will you swear to me that you have never... that you and Domenica have never been lovers?' Marietta turned wild, staring eyes at him.

'Of course. Bring me the Bible. I will swear on that.'

'Ah no,' she laughed bitterly. 'It's easy to swear on the Bible. I want you to swear on something... more powerful.'

'More powerful?'

'Wait here a minute.' Marietta moved across the room faster than she'd moved for months and thrust her arms deep inside a drawer in the oak sideboard. After searching around for a few moments she pulled out a small canvas pouch tied with leather thongs. She brought it over to Pietro.

'Open your hands,' she instructed. When he did, she emptied the contents of the pouch into his open palms.

It was a heap of sandy earth. She closed his fingers over it.

'That is Italian earth,' she said reverently, 'brought with me to England in the hope that one day I would return. I know you will never lie to me on the land of your birth.'

Pietro was speechless. He gripped the small pile of dirt hardly able to believe what was happening.

Why had his wife had kept this earth secretly for years? And for what purpose? Did she often take it out of the drawer and run it through her fingers to make herself feel closer to home? All these questions were unasked and therefore unanswered.

'Now swear to me, on this Italian earth, about you and Domenica. Go on, swear it, if you can!'

He looked her straight in the eye and said in a steady voice, 'I swear to you on this Italian earth that we are not lovers. Domenica and I.'

The tension left her face and she slumped into a chair.

'Thank God!' she whispered. 'Thank God!'

'Did you really think that I would have committed adultery with Domenica -right under your nose?' Pietro could have added *but I've committed adultery in my heart with her since the day I married you.*

'I just wasn't sure,' she said a little nervously, realising she had falsely accused her husband. 'Nello told me that you still loved her. I was so frightened that you would leave me and run away with her. Now that the children have left home… you'd run away and I'd be left all alone.'

'Nello!' he said with scorn. 'You should know by now that he is a big trouble-maker. He's a big drinker too, the man rarely draws a sober breath these days, so how can you take anything he says seriously?'

Marietta had calmed down, all trace of her former hysteria had vanished.

'You're right, Pietro. I'm sorry. And I promise I'll not listen to a word he says in future.'

Pietro's hands were still holding their earthy contents, bits of it escaping through his fingers.

'Open the pouch and I'll pour it back in,' he said.

'No need to,' said Marietta opening her hands to receive the dusty remains. She took it and tossed it through the open window. 'Now that I know the truth about you and Domenica I have no further need of it.'


Marietta decided it would, as Pietro had suggested, be a good idea to go into town and buy herself something nice.

It was a long time since she'd indulged herself. For years it was always the children she put first when handing out the treats. Now that they'd flown the nest she could at least celebrate the fact that they were happy, healthy, independent young people. She and Pietro had done a good job in bringing them up. Yes, she'd mark the occasion by buying a nice piece of gold jewellery perhaps, or a new bonnet. Something extravagant. Pietro could well afford it.

She was happy as she walked to Piccadilly, humming a little Italian tune to herself... a song about love, as most of the Italian songs were. She was lucky, wasn't she...

her husband was faithful and had been all the years of their marriage. Nello had tried to poison her mind about him, hinting at all manner of dreadful things. But last night, Pietro had sworn a solemn oath, on Italian earth – and you couldn't get more solemn than that. And as for the empty nest… it came with its own good points, she was beginning to realise. She wouldn't have to cook large quantities of food everyday… which meant that she could now cook special 'experimental' meals just for the two of them using more expensive, exotic ingredients. Pietro loved his food. She would make him such wonderful meals he would never regret for one moment that he'd married her instead of Domenica!

The driver swore he didn't see the woman walk in front of his horse-drawn tram.

He denied going at an excessive speed – 'how could I in the centre of town?' – and, of course, he was unable to take evasive action because his vehicle ran on fixed tram lines therefore removing the option of swerving round her.

As a result, the woman received the full impact of the collision.

'I shouted out to her but she seemed in a dream,' he kept repeating, very much in distress, as he helped the policeman and two passers-by who were struggling to remove the woman's body from beneath the heavy, iron-covered wheels.

# Chapter 26

'Are you going to be able to come to the funeral?' Domenica enquired of her husband who was sitting at the table with his head in his hands.

Nello looked up, his bloodshot eyes focused on her. 'Of course I am, woman!'

His hands began their familiar shaking now they'd nothing sufficiently heavy to hold on to and weigh them down. It was hard to tell whether his red eyes were a result of recent crying or whether he was suffering from his usual alcohol-related condition that had developed through years of heavy drinking.

He reached out and grasped a tumbler of brandy, bringing it precariously to his lips with a trembling hand, downing the contents without spilling too much on the kitchen table. The alcohol calmed him down, as it always did, first thing in the morning.

'We'd better get ready to leave, in that case,' said Domenica. 'I just wanted to make sure you were fit to come.'

'There's nothing wrong with me! I have a slight nervous condition that requires me to take a small amount of brandy for medicinal purposes.'

Nello was sick of his wife going on about his drinking. Not that she actually mentioned the word 'drink'. She wouldn't dare. She wouldn't dare criticise his personal habits. But he only had to see the disgust on her face to know how disapproving she was of his occasional tipple.

Why she had to bring up the subject today, was beyond him. Today of all days! The day they were burying Marietta. His Marietta… the girl he had fallen in love with the moment he set eyes on her. He could hardly believe that she was dead… that he would never see her sweet angel face again. He'd loved her so much… but she had to go and marry Pietro and break his heart! And here was his own wife begrudging him a little drink now and again.

Of course, when it came down to it, it wasn't just now and again. Nello had been drinking hard for years and was now at the stage when he suffered frightening hallucinations.

'The DTs,' Domenica had heard the Irish women call it. *Delirium tremens*, it would seem, was a familiar enough condition among their men. But it was not one that was much talked about in the Italian community. Everyone knew Nello drank a lot, but then so did many other men. Domenica kept the sordid details to herself. She would have felt great shame if everyone knew about Nello's 'blue devils'.

On a bad day, Nello could see them coming down the chimney by the thousand, running around the table, scattering around the house and then out through the keyhole in the back door.

Last night he had his worst-ever attack.

'They're coming down the chimney faster than I can kill them! They're in my pockets, under my collar, in my shoes!' he screamed.

He rushed to the back door and Domenica thought he was going to run out into the alleyway in an attempt to evade his imaginary tormentors. Instead he grabbed a piece of bread from the table and used bits of it to fill in the keyhole in the back door.

'That'll stop them from getting out!' he said wildly.

Then, picking up a big stick from the corner of the room, he started to thrash out.

'I'm killing them! See, I'm killing them!' he yelled out in mad triumph.

Sweeping round with the stick, Nello knocked all the plates and glasses off the kitchen table and sent them flying onto the stone floor.

But, according to Nello, the little blue devils were still coming down the chimney – and faster than he could beat them to death.

'They're getting inside my clothes, inside my shirt, inside my socks!'

Panic took hold of him and he tore off all his clothes.

Domenica stopped him in the nick of time from throwing them in the fire 'to burn the little devils that are hiding there'.


St. Agnes's was crowded when Pietro and his children followed Marietta's coffin into the church.

The funeral Mass had just begun, when there was a commotion from one of the benches. Pietro turned round and was shocked to see Nello standing up and waving his arms around as he noisily pushed his way along the pew and into the aisle where the flower-decked coffin was standing.

The priest stopped mid-sentence and paused while Nello, in full view of the whole congregation, flung himself on Marietta's coffin, sobbing and shouting.

Outspoken displays of grief were to be expected at a funeral, in the priest's experience, particularly at Italian funerals – but they were usually reserved for the grave-side when the loved one was finally committed to the earth and the dramatic words 'ashes to ashes, dust to dust' were pronounced. It was quite unacceptable to have a sacred religious ceremony interrupted in this uncouth, disrespectful manner!

After a time, when Nello didn't appear to be planning on returning to his pew, half a dozen strong young men went over to him.

'Come,' said one of them, 'Let me help you back, then Mass can continue.'

'I'm not going back!' shouted Nello. 'I want to die here with my beloved Marietta! *Dio mio,* can't you understand, all of you, that she was my only reason for living!'

The congregation appeared stunned by the macabre spectacle being enacted in front of them. For Pietro and the children it was a nightmare come true.

Nello just wouldn't be quiet. He wanted to tell them, tell the world, about his love for Marietta and how badly he'd been treated all these years!

'She would have loved *me,* been *my* wife,' he bellowed, his words echoing round the stone walls of the church, 'if *he* hadn't stolen her from me.'

He pointed an accusing finger at Pietro.

'I loved her, I loved her, I loved her!' he sobbed, throwing himself once again across the coffin, knocking the last of the carefully-arranged floral tributes to the ground. 'Come back to me, my Marietta!'

After hesitating initially, stunned with shock, the six young men grappled with Nello and dragged him, struggling and cursing, down the aisle. Thrusting him out of the church they closed the heavy doors firmly behind them. Two of the young men stood guard to make sure he didn't burst in and disrupt the funeral once again.

After banging fruitlessly on the church door for a short time, Nello gave up and staggered home, where he opened yet another bottle of brandy and drank himself insensible.

# Chapter 27

Marietta's sudden death hit Pietro like a bolt from the blue.

'It's the shock,' he kept saying. 'She was only shopping in town! How can you die doing that?'

What he didn't mention – and could barely acknowledge even to himself – was the guilt. Guilt for all the years of their marriage when he had wished that, instead of Marietta, he'd had Domenica as his wife.

Pietro was filled with self-loathing and pain. Pain seemed to stretch from his abdomen to his throat. If he could have his time again there were so many things he would have done differently.

Pietro kept himself busy in the weeks and months following Marietta's death by making a headstone for her grave.

He put his heart and soul into it. It was going to be one of the most beautiful monuments in the Catholic cemetery, he vowed, and it would be his last major sculpture. From now on, he decided, all new commissions would be done by his sons who were well able to take on Pietro's share of the business.

When the monument was installed, only then did he feel he was able to say goodbye to Marietta – and his guilt. Goodbye to the girl who had saved his sanity by coming into his life and loving him when he needed it the most.

He worked, fashioning the *bianchi marmi* into a scene of angels and cherubim with Marietta's name spelled out in gold inlaid letters.

Soon, he would put all his affairs in order. With Marietta gone – and with Nello and Domenica on his doorstep – he couldn't bear to live any longer in his adopted land. There were just too many reminders of the mistakes he'd made in the past. He needed the restorative air and comfort of his homeland. Soon, he would book his passage to Italy.

# Epilogue

It was two years since Marietta's death.

Returning home to Fizzano to the farm where he was born had been the best thing he could have done, under the circumstances.

And yet, the welcome he'd received from his Italian family, their warm compassion and tender loving care, could not obliterate his feelings of isolation, of being cut off from the rest of mankind.

Perhaps moving into his new villa, presently being built on a nearby plot of land, would make him feel less lonely. Would being on his own, he wondered, be better than being surrounded by generations of Falgonis? The fact that they all appeared to be happy and contented only emphasised his own solitary situation.

Pondering these thoughts, he strode out across his brother's fields and vineyards to his own building plot.

It was September and the land was wreathed in banks of mists that floated through the valley in the early morning. The air was refreshingly cool. Later in the day the sun would break through the misty clouds burning them away, revealing the rich, deep colours of the late summer landscape.

The foundations of his new house had been laid, and the walls of the downstairs rooms were coming along well. He checked the work every day – he'd worked long enough with stonemasons and builders to know that you got a better job done if the workers knew you were watching their every move.

As he walked alone he allowed himself to think sometimes of the past, and of what he'd left behind in England. The fast pace of life, the magnificent buildings he'd worked on and which now stood as monuments to his art – but most of all he thought about the people he'd left behind. He missed his children very much, but it was only natural to let the next generation do things their own way and to have control of the business. And, of course, the whole idea of building this large villa was so that all his children and, in time, his children's children could come over and stay with him for extended holidays, or even to live there with him. So it wasn't as if he would never see them again.

The one person he forced himself *not* to think about was Domenica. Three months ago, he had received news from England.

'Nello has died,' Pietro's eldest son wrote.

'He went a terrible yellow colour, a fever of the liver they said, and soon afterwards took to his bed and never recovered. Domenica is as well as can be expected.'

Pietro crossed himself and prayed that Nello's soul would rest in peace.

He arrived at the building site before the workmen. He liked to do that, checking on everything while no-one else was around. It also gave him a chance to imagine how it would be when the house was finished and he was living there.

He surveyed the scene before him.

The fields of corn ready for harvest, the vines heavy

with black grapes that were veiled with a purple bloom, and the green grapes shining like polished jade. On the slopes behind the farm were the olive trees, the last to emerge from the morning mist.

The colours of the September countryside were deeper and richer than in the burning hot days of summer, with a depth and brilliance about them. It was so beautiful, so very beautiful, and yet it did not mean as much to him as he'd imagined it would.

'What is it you want?' he asked himself out loud. But he was unable to supply the answer.

A movement in the distance caught his attention. It was a woman dressed in black emerging from the olive grove. Probably a local countrywoman out collecting mushrooms for her family.

He turned and walked back to his half-built house. Then he heard his name called.

Looking round, he saw that the woman was moving towards him. Hurrying, and calling his name.

For a fleeting second, a fear took hold of him. Had something happened to his elderly parents back at the farm?

The fear left him as quickly as it came when he recognised who it was calling through the morning mist. He stood transfixed, making no move towards her. The years fell away as he knew it was the woman he'd fallen in love with on a hot summer's day in Fizzano.

The gap was closing between them. He ran to her, and when he reached her he lifted her up, swinging her round as he would a small child.

Her arms wrapped around his neck and she clung to

him.  'I've come home, Pietro,' she said. 'Where I belong… with you.'

As if it had been waiting for that moment, the sun broke through the clouds.  And the last hot rays of the Tuscan summer sun warmed their backs as they held one another close to their hearts.

Printed in Great Britain
by Amazon